I0688657

SECONDHAND
SOLDIER

MICHELE E. GWYNN

AN M.E. GWYNN PUBLICATION

Copyright © 2019 by MICHELE E. GWYNN

All rights reserved.

This story is a work of fiction. All characters, settings, and situations are products of the author's imagination and in no way are representative of or related to real persons. No portion of this book may be reproduced in any form without written permission from the publisher or author, except as permitted by U.S. copyright law.

GET A FREE BOOK

Get a FREE BOOK (or two) from Michele E. Gwynn. See my website for details. Visit micheleegwynnauthor.com today!

Like FREE audiobooks? Check out my YouTube channel and enjoy full length audiobooks from my Harvest Trilogy (Sci-Fi) and Angelic Hosts series (Romantic Fantasy), and more. More coming soon in my military romance series. SUBSCRIBE to my YouTube channel to receive alerts when I upload the next free audiobook. (And share this info with your audiobook-loving friends). Visit my YouTube channel at @MicheleEGwynnAuthor.

Cover by Emeegee Graphics, Cover photo by Jakob Owen (Unsplash), and DC National Mall photo by Casey Homer (Unsplash)

Editing: M.E. Gwynn

CONTENTS

PROLOGUE

Ash fell from the tip of the cigarette burning down to the butt. The man watched it scatter as it landed on the table. He picked up the glass tumbler before him and knocked back the last of the vodka. It was good. The real stuff. Not like the second-rate brands back home. A hint of honey coupled with the heat of pepper combined creating a flavor all its own that slid over his palate slick and clean. He sighed.

"Is good, Da?"

He nodded at the man sitting across from him. "It is. I miss it. I miss us, uncle. It's good to be back home." Alexei felt the warmth of the vodka suffuse his body relaxing his limbs. He looked around the small kitchen. It looked exactly as he remembered it. Yellowed floral wallpaper now peeling at the corners, oak cabinets and countertops, and a stone hearth in the corner. The antique oak table where he sat had not changed. It was surrounded by spindle-back chairs that had seen better days, but his Yaya still kept the dining set polished. At the age of five, he would sit here while his grandmother, Olga Kolysnikova, cooked big dinners for the family. Back then, the man sitting across from him, Sergei Kolysnik, was only a child himself, the youngest brother of his own mother, Anna. Sergei was only three years older than Alexei and the two grew up almost as brothers rather than uncle and nephew. When Anna and her husband Demetri defected to the United States during the early eighties, she left her family behind becoming a great shame in the eyes of their grandfather, a major in the Russian army. It wasn't until years after President Reagan's famous speech to Mikhail Gorbachev demanding he "tear down that wall," that she was able to reach out to them once again. It was with news of his father's passing following a car accident in Las Cruces, New Mexico. Two people died that day, his father, and a woman driving the other car, the one that hit him.

Alexei was surprised at the warm reception he received from his long-lost family, but they remained cold towards his mother until the day she died three years past from a heart attack. He was already in the army then, a decorated soldier who'd received the Purple Heart for saving three brothers in arms from an insurgent attack in Afghanistan. He'd been shot up badly in the effort. Bullets riddled his left side shredding his arm and shattering the bones in his leg. The men he helped save got him to safety, but by then, infection had set into the wounds. The surgeons did all they could to save his limbs, but in the end, gangrene set in and they had to amputate both to save his life. He'd been sent to Nevada for specialized rehabilitation. It lasted more than a year. He'd grown stronger, found new purpose, but the damage to his mind, to his spirit led to a bitterness he could not overcome. Still, he followed orders which now and again brought him to Russia where he was able to visit his family. It was the only thing that kept him whole.

"It is good to see you, nephew. We have missed you." Sergei refilled Alexei's glass.

Sipping the cold liquor, Alexei smiled. "Pulling the uncle card, I see. And your English has improved too," he chuckled.

"My English has always been passing, but your Russian stinks. You've forgotten so much." Sergei sat back and eyed his nephew noting the cigarette held in Alexei's hand had burned down to the butt. "You're burning your hand."

Alexei glanced down. He sent a thought to the hard metal that was his prosthetic arm and the hand lifted shifting to dump the nearly-burnt-out stub into the ashtray. "It won't hurt it. Nothing does. American ingenuity at its best," he said, forming a fist and slamming it down onto the wooden surface of the table.

Sergei reached out, laughing. "Careful. Grandmother may be a tiny pile of wrinkles and arthritic joints, but she can still whip you if you damage her tabletop."

Alexei grinned thinking of the old woman who'd welcomed him with open arms. "And I wouldn't wish to make her angry. My apologies." His metal hand relaxed as his flesh and blood right hand reached again for the tumbler. He sipped the drink, breathing in the aroma. "I don't remember the vodka being this strong before. Either that or I'm just used to the piss-poor brands back home." His words slurred slightly as he settled deeper into the spindle-back chair.

"Americans can't make proper vodka," said Sergei. "Now, tell me again about all the fancy tricks this thing can do." He tapped a finger on Alexei's metal arm. "Entertain me, soldier boy."

In the back of his mind, Alexei knew he was not to reveal anything about the technology behind his prosthetic limbs, but Sergei was family, and he was so far from America. His uncle probably wouldn't even understand, what with being a desk-jockey for a government accounting office. He was a glorified secretary, not a soldier. Alexei rolled up his sleeve and, letting the world fall away, showed Sergei the wonders of science and regaled him with a few stories from the field where he'd put that science to use.

By the end of the night, Alexei and Sergei had finished off an entire bottle of vodka and the fire in the hearth had burned low. Rising from his seat, Sergei reached out to touch his nephew's hair. The younger man was sound asleep with his head resting on his folded arms, his body slumped onto the table.

"I'm sorry, nephew," he whispered. Gently, he pulled Alexei's arm from beneath his face as he lifted and resettled him in the chair. He removed his nephew's shirt and then his pants leaving him in his underwear. After he positioned Alexei just right under the overhead light, he pulled a small camera from his pocket. Sergei Kolysnik began taking picture after picture from every angle. He took measurements, and when he was finished, he lifted Alexei in his arms and carried him into the small bedroom off the kitchen. He laid him on the twin bed and placed a thick cover over him, tucking his nephew in. It would be hours before the drugs wore off, just enough time to deliver the information to the Kremlin and get back home.

CHAPTER 1

Hot air blasted Eastwood's face from the moment he was taken off the C-5 Galaxy. The flight from Ramstein was long and fraught with crazy bouts of unconsciousness. He'd lost time. The two nurses aboard had said very little in between making sure his IV was fed a cocktail that could knock out a horse, and he found their closed-mouthedness frustrating. He remembered asking twice where they were taking him. Once when one of the nurses showed up in his hospital room with a paramilitary escort—a couple of over-muscled dicks who'd unhooked his monitors and then unceremoniously lifted him onto a gurney despite his protests and grunts of pain, and again at the airstrip leaving out of Ramstein. Both times he'd been shut down quickly and drugged into silence.

By the time he'd awoken mid-flight he was royally pissed off, confused from the sedatives, and in pain. He knew if he asked again, he'd just get the needle full of nighty-night juice, so he kept his mouth shut and observed his surroundings through narrowed eyes. From what he could gather, the paramilitary dicks were hired mercenaries. One of the two glared at him and the other men on the gurneys, the hostility rolling off him in waves. He wore a camo jacket with the sleeves rolled up revealing a black snake tattoo wrapped around his right wrist. The other one wore his hair long and tied back. He ignored the patients, keeping his distance. Their mannerisms bespoke their previous military background, but their appearance showed a parting of ways with chain-of-command and regulations. He'd met these types before out in the field. Blackwater blokes hired by foreign governments to infiltrate and rein in rogue factions and take out the opposition. They killed for money, so what they hell were they doing here?

The interior of the C-5 was massive, one of the largest military transport aircraft available, but the cabin area was occupied solely by the two nurses and two mercenaries who kept an eye on not only Eastwood, but two other wounded soldiers. One had black hair with bandages covering his right eye and more wrapped around his right hand. Eastwood could see there were a couple fingers missing. The other was a blond male. His right arm was gone. Both were unconscious, probably still under the effects of the knock-out cocktail administered by the nurses.

Although he'd tried to listen for any tidbit of information, none was forthcoming. It was as if he'd entered some bizarre twilight zone where no one spoke. A beep to his right alerted him to a pump attached to his IV. Eastwood noted the machine now pumping fluid into his line. The sedative hit hard and fast.

"Aw, fuck this shi..." Disturbing dreams plagued his rest. The loud whistle of an incoming RPG. The explosions that knocked him out of his hospital bed at Base Camp 10 inside Kuwait. His buddy, Doc, and the nurses, Leisl Craig and Angie Nelson immediately going to work applying a tourniquet to his leg. Damn-near the entire hospital had been wiped out before the attack by ISIS insurgents was stopped. He didn't remember much after that. He'd awakened to discover his lower left leg gone and life as he knew it—over. The despair, a lingering remnant of the dream, was the last thing he remembered before the blast of hot air engulfed him. A new medical team arrived when the C-5 landed. They wheeled his gurney down the ramp to the tarmac. He glanced around. There was nothing but miles and miles of desert in every direction.

"Where the fuck am I? Where've you taken me? Is this Kuwait? Iraq?"

A tall black woman wearing a scowl and the insignia of major approached. Eastwood noticed a slight limp, but it was the scar above her left eye that drew his attention before his hand automatically lifted in salute.

"Sergeant Tyler," she said, acknowledging the gesture, "I'm Major Sydelle Maxwell, your new commanding officer. Welcome to Camp Lazarus."

"Ma'am," he said, a look of confusion crossing his face, "I'm sorry, but I've never heard of Camp Lazarus. Where, exactly, am I?"

"No one has, Sergeant. You're in Nevada, Area 51, to be precise. This is where you'll be rehabilitated. The army has invested a great deal in you, Harold Tyler. It's time to get a return on that investment. You will do as I say, when I say, and you will work hard. There is no turning back. But first, you'll be turned over to the medical team to get you back on your feet."

Eastwood's eyes popped. "My feet? I only have one, Major—"

"Don't interrupt!" she barked. "After they get you back on your feet, you're mine. That's when the hard work begins, do you understand?"

"No, I can't say that I do," he mumbled.

Major Maxwell's scowl increased deepening the scar over her left eye. "Good. Welcome to PATCH-COM, Sergeant." She gave a pointed look to the medical team who began once again wheeling the gurney towards a hospital bus.

Eastwood could only watch, flabbergasted, as the other two patients from the C-5 were brought in behind him, their gurneys locked securely into place. The scene was surreal. He was in Nevada, in Area 51, a military site historically obscured beneath a deliberate cloud of mystery to hide top secret weapons testing, combat aircraft, and battlefield hardware development, and it was real. PATCH-COM was real. What. The. Fuck?

The bus ride lasted all of fifteen minutes before it pulled to a stop outside of a concrete structure in the shape of a dome built into the side of a mountain. The dome parted in the center, the two halves sliding back on massive rails revealing an opening wide enough to drive a bus through. The bus driver threw the engine into gear and did just that. Behind them, the thick concrete dome walls closed, the massive structures rumbling like a freight train on the steel tracks, obliterating the sunlight and plunging them into darkness. The bus proceeded down a ramped tunnel illuminated by amber lights recessed into the roof. Eastwood felt the world falling away as they descended into the earth. They must've driven thirty feet down by his best guess before the ramp ended in a wide-open space bustling with activity.

Uniformed personnel walked around golf-cart sized vehicles weaving in and out of tunnels branching out from the main floor where the bus parked. It was a military base buried deep into the Nevada desert, one of which the general public was unaware existed, although conspiracy theorists had suspected all along. *Little did they know, they were right*, thought Eastwood. He looked up at a sign posted above the largest of the branch tunnels. It read, WELCOME TO CAMP LAZARUS-WHERE THE DEAD RISE.

Eastwood's eyebrows shot up. "Fucking Twilight Zone shit."

"Twilight Zone?" a groggy voice said.

Eastwood looked left at the man in the gurney next to his. The bandage over the man's eye was thick, but the unbandaged hazel eye staring back at him was filled with confusion. "Yeah. Where we are right now, man. It's like some crazy shit straight out of Rod Serling's imagination."

"I thought I was going to a rehab hospital. Why is it so dark?" The younger man looked around.

"So did I. And we're underground. That's why it's so damned dim in here."

The man pulled himself up on one elbow, a grimace of pain contorting his face. "Did you just say we're underground?" He looked out the bus window taking it all in. "Where are we?"

Eastwood grunted. "The million-dollar question. Camp Lazarus, also known as fucking Area 51 in Nevada."

One black eyebrow shot up. "Shut the fuck up!"

"No lie, man. I met our new C.O. on the way in. Major Maxwell. She didn't look or sound like she was kidding."

The man paused, shaking his head. "I'm sorry, but this all sounds crazy."

"I'm aware. Still trying to wrap my head around it too. I'm Harold, by the way. Harold Tyler, U.S. Army Green Beret, Colorado unit. My friends call me Eastwood." He extended his hand.

The other man reached out, shaking it. "Art Diaz, Corporal, Marines. Nice to meet you, Eastwood. Is that some Dirty Harry reference?"

Eastwood chuckled. "It is. Just too much of a mouthful to use in the field. I'm a weapons specialist. Or...was."

"Are. You are a weapons specialist. You never lose that." Art made a face. "Well, unless you're a fucking sniper with no eye. Then maybe you lose your specialty."

"You still have one good one, man," Eastwood offered.

Art rolled his one good eye and glanced down at Eastwood's body. "And you still have one good leg, I guess. Fucking broke dicks, that's what we are."

"Two, man. Two good legs. One to stand on to take a piss and the other to keep the ladies happy."

Art laughed. "Because the ladies just love secondhand soldiers, right?"

"You two done strokin' each other or can a dying man get some peace and quiet?"

Eastwood and Art looked over at the third gurney. The blond man lay wiping his eyes with his one and only hand.

"Well, shit, the dead has arisen," said Eastwood.

"Like Lazarus," said Art.

"It's Matt. Rogers. Not Lazarus. What kind of biblical bullshit is that anyhow?"

"I'm Art, and that's Eastwood, and we don't know yet," said Diaz. Two medical aides entered the bus and moved in their direction. "But I think we're about to find out."

CHAPTER 2

Eastwood, Art, and Matt were taken to a hospital wing deep inside the maze of tunnels. The amazed sergeant was sure he'd never be able to find his way back out into the sunlight again without a trail of breadcrumbs. The two aids that took them off the bus were joined by a third aid, a quiet young man who avoided eye contact. No questions were answered beyond assuring them they would soon be in their private rooms.

Eastwood soon found himself inside a small room with a hospital bed, a private bathroom, a flat screen television on the wall, a combination closet/dresser, and a stainless-steel chair in the corner. There were no windows and the light switches on the wall were labeled DAYLIGHT and NIGHTLIGHT. When he asked, the quiet young man said, "The daylight switch offers the UV spectrum of the sun to compensate for being underground and the nightlight is the usual amber lighting you'd have in your lamps at home. It helps you to regulate your circadian rhythm so you can sleep."

Art was taken next door and Matt was wheeled across the hall. The three men weren't the only ones in the wing. There were four more rooms in their hall. The sounds of television and general movement indicated the rooms were occupied. Eastwood took it all in as the aid helped transfer him to his new bed. After securing his leg in the trapeze to alleviate swelling, the quiet young soldier explained the panel buttons on the bedside.

"This one controls the television. The volume and channel buttons are here and here," he said, pointing. "Next to that is a control for your lighting. You can turn it all on from here and even dim the nightlight to your preference. And this button, the red one, is the nurse call bell. If you need assistance with going to the bathroom or need pain meds and stuff, that's the button. Someone should be in shortly to get you set up and dinner is in an hour." The young man turned to leave, joining the other two aids in the hall. Their footsteps echoed, the sound fading slowly into the distance.

In the near silence, with nothing better to do, Eastwood turned on the TV. There were movie channels, streaming, sports, but no local or national news channels. There was no real-time link to the outside world. There was also no phone and he didn't see his duffel bag anywhere. He was cut off and pissed off. He eyed the red button, then pressed it. When nothing happened, he hit it again. Thirty seconds went by before he hit it again, growing angrier.

The click-clack sound of high heels slapped out a staccato beat on the concrete floor of the hallway getting louder as they approached his door. Eastwood glared at the opening waiting for the nurse to appear. He was ready to rip some-one a new one and the slow-to-respond nurse would have to do. He opened his mouth to bark his displeasure and froze.

"I knew you'd be a problem, but I didn't think it would be so soon."

He knew that honeyed voice. Knew the smirk on her red lips, the gold in her silky hair, and the curvature of the hip her hand rested on as she stood, one foot inside the doorway. She huffed and her luscious breasts heaved. He knew those too. Intimately. Knew the feel of them in his hand, their weight in his palms, the taste of them on his tongue. She raised a blonde eyebrow. "What's the matter, Harry? Cat got your tongue?"

Joely Winter approached his bedside, amusement lighting her big, blue eyes. Memories of their night together in London came flooding back. It was nearly a year ago when they'd met. Her friend Emma's thirtieth birthday took a dangerous turn when she was kidnapped by an international terrorist. It was his team, led by Outlaw, that rescued her, and then damned if she didn't get taken a second time by the same lunatic jihadist. Emma was now Outlaw's wife and soon-to-be mother of their first child, but in the middle of all the craziness was his night with Joely. As he recalled, she was some kind of genius bio-tech prodigy who'd invented a prosthetic for athletic amputees or some shit. He hadn't really been paying much attention to anything outside of noticing how hot she was, and then he'd snaked her away from Hollywood who'd been too drunk at the time to notice. He was sure she hadn't minded that at all. Hollywood had attached himself to her early on at the nightclub and Joely had been too nice to tell his buddy to fuck off.

She didn't tell him to fuck off though. Nope. The hot blonde bombshell had taken his hand and led him straight to paradise. She fucked like a champion and to his surprise, was up front about it being a one-night stand. A London fling, she called it. Hell, she'd even thanked him afterward...for his service. It tickled him then, her forthright manner and brutal honesty. That was before Emma had gone missing. Funny, although he'd enjoyed their hook-up, he hadn't thought about her since. Not much, anyhow. Maybe a little, he admitted to himself. But what was the point in hankering over a woman he knew he'd never see again, both because of his job and because she'd straight-out labeled their intensely sweaty fuck-fest a hit-and-run? None. The answer was none. But now, here she was, in this underground military facility, and he wanted to know why.

"My tongue is just fine, as I'm sure you'll remember," he said. "You want to tell me just what the hell is going on? Why are you here? Why, Joely, am I here?"

Joely sauntered to his bedside and placed a well-manicured hand lightly upon his left knee. She glanced below her hand to the white-bandaged stump, all that remained of that leg. "I'm here to give you back your leg, Harry. To help rebuild you."

He felt the heat of her soft hand on his skin and his body reacted despite his anger and confusion. "Explain," he said, voice dropping low.

Joely smiled, her thumb caressing his knee absently. "My company is now contracted with the military. My prosthetics have been modified for combat soldiers so that good men like yourself live to fight another day. The military considers you a valuable investment, one they don't want to lose, so they're investing in you again. That's where WinRunner comes in. You probably remember I designed prosthetics for athletes," she said, raising a questioning eyebrow.

Eastwood grunted, "Something like that, yeah." The pleasant sensation of her hand on his knee sent tingles up towards his groin erasing the continual pain he'd felt since the explosion better than morphine ever could. He cleared his throat, determined she wouldn't get away with charming him out of his anger. He focused on her lips, watching them form words. Big mistake.

"Well, as I told you in London, somewhere between the sheets, the military came calling. I'd already entered into contract with them and we'd been developing the new, exclusive line of military-grade prosthetics by then."

"You mean this place existed then?" He pulled his thoughts from the image of her nude body stretched out upon fancy London sheets.

"Oh, yes. Long before I came along, PATCH-COM existed. I don't know exactly for how long, but I've only been part of R&D for two years."

He digested her words. "You said something about giving me my leg back?"

Joely nodded, sadness coloring her eyes a deeper shade of blue. "Yes. When I saw your name on the intake list, it broke my heart." She squeezed his thigh; her hand having crept up an inch. "I couldn't believe it. I know it was just a one-nighter, but we did share that night together, Harry. It hurt me seeing that this had happened to you. You're so strong and fearless and confident."

Eastwood was taken aback by her compliment. But it was the pain in her eyes that surprised him most. "Hey," he said, reaching out for the first time to cover her hand with his own, "I'm okay. I'll be okay."

Joely sighed, swallowing hard before regaining her composure. "I know. I know because I'm going to make it so. My team and I have already created your new leg. Come tomorrow, you'll be fitted properly, and your rehabilitation begins. We're going to get you up not only walking again, Harry, but running. Stronger than ever before. You can count on it."

He looked at her, standing before him with a determination that matched the hope written all over her beautiful face. How could he stay angry? Why was he angry at all, at least, at her? She'd done nothing but happen to be here.

He lifted her hand to his lips, placing a soft kiss on her knuckles. "Then I won't let you down."

She smiled, and then gently pulled her hand away. "But no hanky-panky," she admonished, shaking a red-tipped fingernail in his face. "There's no fraternizing between personnel here. Hard rule, so get used it. You'll have to take care of that," she said, pointing at the evidence of his desire, "...on your own." She turned to leave, then glanced over her shoulder. "But I'm happy to see it still stands at attention when I walk into the room." With that, she strolled out, deliberately swishing her hips for his appreciative gaze.

"Damn," he said, chuckling low. "But when have I ever followed the rules?"

CHAPTER 3

The gymnasium was a sight to behold. The cavernous room was filled with every high-tech piece of equipment one could imagine. Cardio machines, free weights, rowing machines, aquatic treadmills, a pool, a track around the perimeter, bikes, a rock-climbing wall, ropes hanging from the ceiling, a cargo net like the ones used on army obstacle courses. In one corner were mats and therapy tables currently occupied by other patients working with their therapists. An aid wheeled Eastwood to a station on the far-left side. There was a large worktable next to a therapy bed. Upon the table stood something best described as a prop from any *Terminator* movie. The metallic leg rested in a stand. The polished nickel appearance of the metal did not reflect the light around it as many metals would. Instead, it seemed to absorb and diminish it. No glare. No shine. Strange, yet compelling.

"What's this?" he said, reaching out to touch the stand as the aid, a young private, locked the brakes on his wheelchair.

"That," said a voice from behind, "is your new leg."

A man appeared coming around Eastwood's right side. He had salt-and-pepper hair going thin on top and dark-rimmed, government-issued glasses. Of medium height, he had an impressive set of shoulders and arms that clearly said he worked out. He extended a hand.

"I'm Joe Poole, your therapist."

"Sergeant Harold Tyler," said Eastwood, gripping Joe's hand.

"Good to meet you, Sergeant." Joe returned his attention to the prosthetic. "This piece of art was specially crafted for you. The engineers have been working on it for five days now getting the dimensions just right. Now it's my turn to fit you and get the inside adjusted to your stump."

Eastwood blinked. "A week?"

Joe nodded. "Yes, I believe so."

His eyes narrowed and brow creased as Eastwood processed that information. It was five days past that he'd been injured in the blast back at Base Camp 10 in Kuwait.

He'd only found out about coming to rehab a day and a half ago. How the hell could anyone here at Camp Lazarus have known about his leg, much less begun to work on a prosthetic any sooner than that? Something wasn't right.

"And who is this engineering team?" he asked.

Joe lifted the leg off the stand. "Dr. Winter and her team. I can arrange a meeting if you like."

"We've met, Joe. Harry and I go way back."

Eastwood whipped his head around at the sound of her soft voice. Joely stood just to his left, one hand now resting on his shoulder. She wore a white pencil skirt that outlined her curvy hips and a red blouse that matched her lips. Her legs were accented by the strappy red high heels on her delicate feet. In all, she looked amazing, but the anger simmering inside him labeled her a she-devil, one who knew something he didn't. And he intended to find out exactly what the hell was going on.

"Dr. Winter is it?" The skepticism in his tone barely concealed.

She smiled, rubbing his shoulder. "Yes, I have a doctorate in biomedical engineering."

"Is that so?"

"Yes. It's a fact. I can show you the parchment. It's hanging in my office." She cocked her head, watching him carefully.

Joe coughed. "If you're ready, Sergeant, let's have a look at your leg and then we'll try this prosthetic on."

Eastwood tamped down his suspicion and anger and focused on the therapist. "Sure." He reached down to unlock the chair, beating the Private to it. He shooed him away. "I got this!"

Joe glanced sideways at the Private. "I'll call you when his time here is finished. Dismissed."

Eastwood rolled the chair back and away from the table giving Joe access to his leg. It was propped up on pillows that cushioned the chair's leg extension. Joe pulled up a rolling stool and sat, scooting in. He set the prosthetic on the floor and reached out to feel around Eastwood's left knee and further down.

A hiss from the patient made him stop.

"Still tender?" Joe touched the bandaged stump gently.

"Yeah." Eastwood replied, his face stoic but his eyes narrowed in pain.

"Did you get your meds this morning?"

He shook his head. "Didn't need them. I don't take drugs unless I'm dying."

Joe bit his lip, glancing over Eastwood's head at Joely. "Well, you're going to regret that shortly. This is going to hurt. Tomorrow take the meds. Today, you'll have to suck it up, soldier."

"I can handle it," said Eastwood. Even to his own ears it sounded petty, like he was trying to convince himself. He didn't like to appear weak, to anyone for any reason. He especially didn't like it that she was here to witness it. Weakness was a disadvantage he couldn't afford. He needed answers and to get them, he needed to be in a position of strength. No matter what happened over the next hour, he would not show weakness. Pain was his immediate enemy and he'd be damned if pain would win. "Let's do this."

Joe began to unwrap Eastwood's leg. When it was uncovered, he saw what was left of his own flesh laid bare for the first time. It was devastating. The stump was swollen still, and the seam where his skin was sewn back together stretched tight. The thought of putting it into the prosthetic made him cringe. Especially when he glanced down seeing into the top of the metal leg. The opening didn't look big enough.

Joe pulled a stocking out of a new wrapper. "This sock goes on first. Ready?"

Eastwood took a deep, steadying breath. "Yeah."

The therapist rolled the sock back and placed it on the end of the stump. Eastwood gritted his teeth, taking slow breaths. He felt every inch of the stocking as it was pulled up over his sensitive skin. When it was over his knee and tugged tight one last time, he exhaled. Soft hands massaged his shoulders, a reminder he had an audience.

"You're doing great, Harry," she said.

Her scent tickled his nose, vanilla today. It made him think of cookies. He loved cookies. Doc's mom's cookies came to mind. She was a chef who made the best cookies he'd ever tasted, outside those of his own mom, Meredith Tyler. He wondered what his teammate was up to now, where he and the rest of the team were in the world? What new mission were they running? He hoped his friend had finally told the feisty, red-headed nurse how much he cared about her because it was obvious to anyone with eyes the idiot was in love. Last he knew, Leisl had pulled through surgery and Doc was rushing to her side. He figured there'd be another wedding to attend soon. Last one was Outlaw's, his team leader. Well, former team leader. He'd been reassigned without so much as a by-your-leave, and to what, he still couldn't grasp. A unit of broke dicks? Physically disabled soldiers without a leg to stand on. It was absurd, but his thoughts kept him distracted until the moment Joe Poole shoved a vice onto his stump.

"Ow! Fuck, that hurts!" Eastwood kicked out with his good leg catching Joe off-guard and sending him flying backwards. The therapist landed on his back, air rushing from his lungs from the impact.

"Joe!" Joely rushed forward, dropping down to her knees at his side. "Are you okay?"

Poole chuckled. "My fault. I should've warned him." He threw a look at Eastwood who sat panting, nostrils flared, contrition flashing in his green eyes.

"Sorry, man."

Joe got up, once again sitting down on the stool. "Told ya you'd be sorry." He scooted closer as Joely rose keeping clear of Eastwood's good leg. "That's a helluva kick you've got. Worse than a damned mule."

"And twice as stubborn," said Joely.

Irritation replaced the contrition in his eyes. He didn't like losing control.

"How's it feeling," asked Joe.

"It's throbbing like a bitch." Eastwood swallowed, focusing all his energy on controlling his breathing once again.

"That's normal. Your stump is still swollen, but when the swelling goes down, you'll begin to feel better. Wearing the prosthetic will help with forcing the excess fluids up and out your lymph glands at the inner thigh. You ready to stand up?"

Green eyes popped wide. "What? Now?"

"All you need to do today is stand for a moment, as long as you can manage. After that we'll prop your leg up and leave the prosthetic on for an hour while we do some upper body workout." Joe stood and reached for Eastwood's arm.

He waved off Joe's helping hand. "I can do it. I've been standing all my life."

"It's not the same—"

Joe threw Joely a look that said, '*Let him try.*'

Locking the wheels on his chair, Eastwood pulled the levers swinging the foot pedals out to the side, left leg last as Joe held the prosthetic before carefully lowering it to the floor. Blood rushed to the stump causing the throbbing to turn into a violent pounding at the incision site. He swore he felt real pain in his shin and foot, but that was impossible because he no longer had a shin or a left foot. His logical brain said the pain wasn't real, but the illogical portion of his brain said "*Stop, you fucking idiot! This hurts!*" He moved to the edge of the seat and placed his hands on the armrests, pushing up. Leaning heavily on his right leg, he stood, slowly rising. It was shaky at best.

"Okay, good," said Joe. "Now, try and get fully upright and shift your weight more to the left until it's evenly distributed." He stood at Eastwood's side, ready to grab him at a moment's notice.

Eastwood sucked air through gritted teeth, his face showing the strain. It felt like he'd never stood up in his life. Slowly, he let his left leg take a little more of his weight. A high-keening sound escaped his lips. His left thigh and knee screamed in pain and his body grew shaky. Grunting, he let the leg take half his weight, powering through. His entire body was rigid with effort. He'd done it. He'd stood up on the new prosthetic leg. He glanced at Joely. She smiled and clapped her hands, applauding his Herculean effort.

"Told you I could do it," he said, jaw clenched. A bead of sweat trickled down over his eye. As soon as the words passed his lips, his body collapsed, listing sideways. Joe caught him and used the momentum to guide him back into the wheelchair.

"Goddammit!" Eastwood cursed a blue streak. He'd never felt such pain, not even when his leg had been blown off by an RPG blast. The numbness caused by the trauma had protected him, and later, morphine had blocked the worst of the pain. But this was excruciating. Tomorrow, he'd take the meds offered. He'd take the ones scheduled for the afternoon as well. No more stubborn machismo or else he'd find himself crying like a baby, and that was not going to happen. Damned if he'd let anyone see him cry. Last person to witness that moment of weakness was his mom after he'd broken his arm in the fifth grade falling out of a tree.

A cool, soft hand reached out, wiping the sweat from his forehead with a paper towel. "You're strong as a bull, Harry. I've seen lesser men tear up and cry the first time they stand in a new prosthetic. That was impressive." Joely leaned down, handing the now-folded paper towel to him. "I have to go, but I'll check on you later. I'm proud of you." She straightened and walked away.

Eastwood watched her go, noticing the heads of every broken soldier in the gym turning to follow her progress. His gut clenched and his brow furrowed. He caught Art's eye. The one-eyed man was smiling appreciatively at Joely until he saw the look of murder on Eastwood's face. The smile on Art's face disappeared and he returned his attention to the therapist who tossed a ten-pound medicine ball straight at him. He barely caught it before it hit his face.

Eastwood smirked.

"So how do you and Dr. Winter know each other anyhow," asked Joe. The therapist lifted Eastwood's leg back onto the leg rest, propping the pillows beneath it once again.

"That's classified, Joe."

The man looked at Eastwood, unsure whether he was serious. Shaking his head, he decided to let it go. "Ready for some upper-body work?"

"Can't hurt any worse than what I just did. Let's get this show on the road. Sooner I'm done, the sooner I can get some damned painkillers."

Joe laughed. "It takes a strong man to admit he needs a little help. No shame in that, Sergeant."

"Now you sound like Outlaw."

"He sounds like a wise man."

Eastwood nodded, thinking of his team. He missed them. They'd gone through so much together, and now, he was alone. He wondered if they even knew where the hell he was. Probably not. Somehow, he didn't think many people were in the know about Camp Lazarus, about PATCH-COM. He was only just scratching the surface himself, and he had questions. First question, how the hell did anyone know he'd be coming here five days ago? Second question, why had they brought him here?

CHAPTER 4

Joely read through the file on her desk going over the same paragraph now for the fourth time. She was distracted. Despite her resolve, she couldn't get her mind off a certain green-eyed man. She knew him first as *Eastwood*. That's what his buddies called him, but after he'd taken her hand and they walked to her hotel room in London that night, he'd told her his real name. *Harold*, he'd said. But his friends and family called him Harry, and he'd insisted she should consider herself firmly in the friend category. His forthrightness had made her laugh but the devilish twinkle in his green eyes made her hot and bothered. She wondered where he'd been all night while his teammate, Hollywood, had been slobbering all over her.

When politely disengaging the other one hadn't worked, she'd ordered round after round of shots until Hank 'Hollywood' Jimenez could no longer stand. His friend, Skyscraper, had kept up with Hank shot for shot, but the much taller man held his liquor better, and he hadn't made a nuisance of himself either. Harry, however, kept to the perimeter leaving the way clear for Hollywood, but she'd caught him watching her once or twice. She'd seen the hungry look in his eyes. It wasn't until later, when stepping off the elevator, that he'd made his move. At her doorway, he whispered, *"So why'd you try to give my buddy alcohol poisoning tonight?"*

Joely remembered even now how it felt to be caught between her hotel room door and the large, muscled man with dirty-blond hair and just the hint then of reddish five o'clock shadow. The air between them was charged with heat and electricity, and it excited her.

"It was the only way I could put him out of commission," she'd said.

He chuckled low. "Telling him he's not your type would've been cheaper."

"I agree. I tried that first."

Harry had moved in closer. "Yeah, he's a little thick sometimes, but he's a good guy."

"Is that why you waited? I saw you watching me."

He'd leaned down then, bringing his lips within an inch of hers, his hands still at his sides. "I waited to give my buddy his shot. It's only fair. He saw you first," he said, reaching up to tuck a strand of her blonde hair behind her ear. "And I saw you watching me back. Same look in your eyes then as now, baby. Like what you see?"

The zing that ran through her crashed like a wave low in her belly. Joely remembered that was the moment she'd closed the distance between them, kissing him hard. He returned that kiss in kind, his strong arms wrapping around her waist and lifting her up as he pressed her back up against the door. Her legs snaked around his waist, bringing something solid and promising into direct contact with her now very eager lady parts. She'd fumbled for her keycard, shoving it into the lock and barely getting the door cracked before he forced it open moving towards the bed. He'd thrown her into the middle of it and stood there, pulling off his shirt.

Muscles, tattoos, and scars greeted her voracious gaze. This was a man, a warrior. "Yes, Harry, I do like what I see. Now take off your pants!"

The sex was fantastic, but it was a one-night stand. She refused to get involved with a soldier, especially since she'd recently signed a contract with the military for her company to create prosthetics for a new program. It would be a conflict of interest she couldn't afford. And now, he was here, in the program she'd helped co-create with the Joint Chiefs of Staff over a year ago. Camp Lazarus had been around longer than that, but on the fringe. A ghost. Only a few soldiers had been recycled then, and in a limited way. It was her advanced bio-engineering efforts that allowed the military to continue to get a solid return of their investment in these wounded warriors. For her, it was about rehabilitating these outstanding men and women. She was in awe of their abilities, their knowledge and skill sets, their courage and bravery. For the military, it was about advancing a new branch of special operations to combat enemies in ways they would never suspect.

Syd had been among the first. When Major Maxwell arrived, she was so broken, Joely didn't know if the woman would even survive surgery much less become a candidate for her program. Syd's will was strong, though. She fought through her injuries like a world-class champion. Not a tear fell from her brown eyes nor did she once give up. She used her pain to fuel her determination. The day she first stood unassisted on her new prosthetic leg, after eight months of exhaustive therapy to strengthen her back, was a miracle. After that, nothing stopped her from regaining all her strength and capability. She became the first PATCH after conquering Camp Lazarus's version of Nasty Nick, the obstacle course all special ops had to master before becoming the best of the best, the elite forces.

Joely had been inspired by the woman whom she now called friend and she'd moved forward with the program hoping to recreate that miracle. Army Sgt. Alex Pavluk had been next followed by Petty Officer Nastjia Moreno, the first woman to pass SEAL training. Now she had Ben Holiday, a Green Beret, and Jackson Hicks, a Marine sniper in addition to Art Diaz, Matt Rogers, and her own blast from the past, Sgt. Harold Tyler. Orders were to get them rehabilitated as quickly as possible. Apparently, the military Joint Chiefs didn't stop to think about how long it takes to recuperate from these types of devastating injuries.

In the meantime, she had a job to do and thinking about one hot night with Harry wasn't helping her finish reading this report. She tried again.

It was an intelligence memo, heavily redacted and covered with yellow post-its. She wasn't sure why it was sent to her. She usually wasn't included in any intelligence briefings, but this one felt personal. Angry. Demanding an answer. This one came from a General P.K. Davidson. One post-it stuck out among the rest. *Leak in PATCH-COM?* Joely lifted the note and read the paragraph. *Spec plans for an arm amputee prosthetic with automated weaponry discovered in Ukrainian hotel room in Kiev. Room was registered to REDACTED.*

"What the hell?" She sat back, staring at that line before reading it again. It sank in slowly. Someone in the Ukraine had a prosthetic prototype schematic similar to one of her own. But how?

Joely sat back staring at the crude schematic attached to the report. It was a copy of a copy, hand-drawn with notes written in the Russian Cyrillic alphabet. She had no idea what the actual words were, but she understood their meaning. The image was a rendering of one of her first inventions, one modified by an army weapons specialist. It had since been replaced by two upgrades that only a handful of people knew about. She knew the soldier for whom it had been created well. He was a good guy, quiet mostly. He kept to himself and followed orders without question. He attended his psych sessions weekly and Dr. Lila Delaney's reports showed progress being made with Pavluk's PTSD. Indeed, he'd had not one outburst or incident beyond his third session, having begun utilizing the coping mechanisms Dr. D had introduced.

The weapons specialist, Riddle, was another story. She had no idea what Riddle's full name and rank were since she'd been classified as 'non-essential' for that information. Riddle was an intimidating figure standing at 6'4". He kept his head completely shaved and his blue eyes held no warmth whatsoever. He knew his weapons and he did his job, but beyond that, Joely knew nothing about the man. He'd come in, made the necessary mechanical changes to the arm prosthetic, tested those changes, and then she hadn't seen him again until the second upgrade. She was sure he didn't reside at the base. No one seemed to know who he was or from where he came.

The Joint Chiefs were in the loop along with her own team of assistants, but all her people stayed on base so a leak from any one of them wasn't possible. If it had, indeed, come from one of her own designs, then it came from someone who had the freedom to come and go. That meant only Riddle, Pavluk, and the PATCH team. She would bet her reputation it wasn't anyone from the team. That left Riddle.

Joely quickly fired off her assessment and repackaged the material inside the carrier folder. She marked it PRIORITY and placed it into the outgoing mail file. A runner would pick it up in the morning. It was now out of her hands, and she could focus once again on her work...and maybe try to figure out why it was she couldn't stop thinking about Harry.

CHAPTER 5

Four months passed. For Eastwood, living in the bowels of Area 51 hadn't been nearly as bad as he thought it would be. He'd been given back his cell phone (which didn't work underground) and could call out once a week to his family on a designated landline. Natalie Janeway briefed him on what he could say about where he was when speaking to his mother and other family members. The communications director looked every inch the classic college book nerd, but she was nice, and he couldn't help but like her.

Every Saturday he and his fellow broke dicks were brought into the rec-room where, one by one, they called home. It was a boost to their morale and a shot of adrenaline to their emotions. His mom, Meredith Tyler, was thrilled to hear about his progress. Each week, he had to discourage her from getting on a plane to D.C. where she thought he was hospitalized citing the Pentagon's orders to get him back into shape for re-assignment to an intelligence desk job. Meredith didn't understand why he wasn't being discharged, but she knew her son, knew he would continue to serve, as long as he was able. If the military had plans to keep him and put him behind a desk stateside, she was happy. It meant Harry would be safe, and for that, she was thankful. He promised he'd return home as soon as he was up and running.

For his part, he was surprised to hear from his mother that his old teammate, Doc, had called trying to find out where he was and how he was doing. Why would the military keep his whereabouts a secret from them? They had high-level clearance, at least, Outlaw did. All he'd need to do would be to reach out to General Davidson and ask, or so he thought. Apparently, he was wrong. Still, knowing they hadn't forgotten him brought a smile to his face. In one conversation, he told his mom to tell Doc to "dig a little deeper" and "tell him I ain't dead, just a broke dick." His mom scolded him for his language, making him chuckle, but he knew Doc would understand. Knew he'd know who to ask. He'd thrown a sideways glance at Natalie who sat beside each of them during their conversations to make sure they didn't stray from protocol, but she wasn't looking at him.

He followed her line of sight straight to Diaz. Art was shooting pool with Ben Holiday. The Marine sniper no longer wore gauze bandages wrapped around his head. The eye he'd lost had been replaced by a specialized prosthetic. He couldn't even tell the fake right one from the real one on the left, so concise was the craftsmanship. Despite his improved vision, it seemed Diaz couldn't see the adoring puppy eyes cast his way by Natalie. The young woman had an obvious crush. He, Holiday, and his new buddy, Jackson Hicks, were discussing it only the night before over a game of poker.

"Think he realizes she has the hots for him?" asked Jackson. The laid-back cowboy reminded Eastwood of Doc. Same open, honest personality.

"Fold." Holiday threw down his cards. "It's a shit hand. You cheating, Jackson?"

"I don't need to cheat, Ben. It's just skill," he said.

"Call," said Eastwood. "I don't think ole Art has noticed. Maybe he needs an adjustment on that eye." Eastwood tapped the table.

Jackson laid his cards down revealing a full house. He grinned. "You ain't got a leg to stand on, Harry. Beat that if you can."

Holiday laughed. "He's gonna beat your ass for that leg comment for sure, Jackson."

"You have the same eye malfunction as Diaz if you can't see that coming. Maybe I should start calling you junkyard," said Eastwood, kicking the modified titanium exoskeleton brace around Jackson's right leg."

"My eye sees just fine, thank you. Want me to pull it out and show ya?" Jackson laughed, reaching for his left eye.

"For fuck's sake, no! Keep that creepy shit in your socket where it belongs!" Holiday slapped Jackson's hand down.

"Ain't seen a hole in a while, Ben. I wouldn't want you to get excited and try to skull-fuck me." Jackson sent a thought and a red dot appeared on Ben's crotch.

Alarmed, Holiday jumped back in his chair. "God-dammit, Jackson! Turn off your fucking laser vision!"

Eastwood howled, laughing. "He's right. We're a bunch of weird horny motherfuckers." He put down his cards. "Beat ya. And I didn't cheat."

Jackson's laser sighting disappeared as he focused on the four nines staring back from the tabletop. "Aw, man!"

Holiday snickered, pointing at Jackson. "That's what you get for laser-sighting my dick."

"Be happy anyone paid it any attention, tiny thing that it is."

Eastwood slapped his knee before reaching out to collect the stack of chips he'd won. "That's five hundred dollars you owe me now."

"Maybe you could buy Diaz a clue about the comm director," said Jackson.

"Or," said Eastwood, leaning onto his elbows, "maybe we could have a little side bet. How long before Diaz notices her, and then, double or nothing, how long before he closes the deal?"

"Oh, I like this," said Ben. "Count me in!" He pushed a stack of chips at Eastwood.

Bets had been made, and now, the three waited for results. Still, Eastwood thought, it couldn't hurt to move things along.

"Mom, I gotta go. Time for therapy. Yeah, I love you too. Don't forget what I said to tell Doc. Okay, bye." He hung up. Natalie didn't seem to notice. Eastwood smiled. "Diaz is next, I believe."

"What?" she glanced his way. "Oh, you're finished. Yes, I guess he is next."

Eastwood stood up, now walking easily on his artificial leg. "I'll get him," he said, then leaned down close to her ear. "You know, I shouldn't say this, but I think he likes you." He straightened up and walked to Diaz. "Dude, you're turn." He patted Art on the shoulder, taking the pool cue from him before leaning in to whisper, "Janeway's kinda hot, don't you think?" He moved around the table, joining Holiday in the game.

"What?" Diaz looked from Eastwood to Natalie who now stood, straightening her white button-down shirt over the waist of her black pencil skirt. waiting for him to come and make his weekly call home. A telling blush tinted her creamy cheeks as she noticed Art Diaz's regard.

Eastwood ignored him, leaning down to take a shot. Holiday watched Art throw them a confused look before approaching Natalie.

"I thought we weren't supposed to interfere, man. That's cheating."

"Fuck it. It's fun and I'm bored." Eastwood watched the two.

They both appeared flustered.

Ben Holiday raised a dark eyebrow. His blue eyes twinkled. "You're right, it is fun. Maybe we should kick it up a notch."

"Don't tell Jackson. He's holding the chips."

Major Maxwell entered the room and they stood at attention.

"Gentlemen, in the conference room in five." She turned and left.

Eastwood and Holiday shared a look. Ending his call, Diaz moved past Natalie. In the corner, Matt Rogers put down the book he'd been reading. He stood, joining the others.

"What's going on?" Matt was brought into camp with Diaz, same time as Eastwood. The two had become fast friends.

"I guess we're about to find out," Diaz muttered.

The men fell in line making their way to the conference room two halls overs. Eastwood, Ben, Jackson, Matt, and Art all found their seats at the far end. Sitting at the head of the table was someone new, someone with the rank of Colonel. Major Maxwell stood to his right. Next to her was another man. He was tall, muscled, appearing in his early forties with a crew cut, deep-set blue eyes, and a strong jaw. That man gave off a dangerous vibe, but he seemed contained despite the powder-keg aura. He stared at the tabletop, hands behind his back.

Filling out the next two seats was a petite young woman with black hair pulled into a tight braided bun at the nape of her neck and hostile brown eyes, and a dark-haired soldier with a titanium arm that moved as independently as the other made of flesh and blood. That man's eyes weren't so much hostile as calculating, but neither he nor the woman paid any attention to the far end of the table.

Joely Winter sat in a chair to the left of the Colonel. She looked up, catching Eastwood's eye lingering a moment longer than necessary before clearing her throat and looking away.

He smirked, noting the light-blue silk top she wore with matching slacks. The delicate material of the shirt failed to hide the hardening of her nipples even as she shuffled the small stack of papers in front of her. He wondered if it was the air conditioning or, perhaps, him that caused it. From the second glance she threw his way, he felt sure it was the latter. An answering twinge caused a tightening in his crotch. He clasped his hands casually in front of him. They'd been playing this cat and mouse game for months now. She ignored him for the most part, and he made it clear he wasn't having it. A slow smile spread across his lips, but he suppressed it when Major Maxwell spoke.

"Gentlemen, this is Colonel Ambrose Carnahan. He's from Joint Staff Intelligence. Give him your full attention." Major Maxwell deferred to the Colonel.

Carnahan's dark hair was cut through with threads of steel-gray concentrated at his temples. His dark eyes bore into each one of them. "Have a seat," he said. Everyone took a chair. The Colonel leaned forward, his arms resting on the burnished tabletop. "We have a situation. There's been a recent development in which several spec ops teams have been compromised. While we investigate the leak, we find ourselves in need of a team unknown to anyone at Fort Bragg, a team not listed in the Special Forces database. Gentlemen, that's you."

Eastwood looked at Jackson. Confusion slowly morphed to understanding. For Eastwood, that single line of dialogue explained a lot, but raised even more questions. He knew now why Doc and Outlaw couldn't find him. He no longer existed. They were ghosts. The men on their end of the long table glanced at each other before turning serious eyes back to the Colonel.

"Oddly enough, the mission concerns PATCH-COM," he continued. "One of our agents made a discovery while gathering intelligence on an FSB operative linked to the pro-Kremlin movement in Ukraine. This was found in the operative's hotel room." The Colonel nodded to Major Maxwell who passed out copy to the group. "As you can see, this might look a bit familiar. Too familiar," he said, pinning each man and woman with a hard stare before continuing.

Joely bit her lip, stopping herself from saying something she might later regret. Across from her, the woman with the hostile brown eyes exchanged a glance with the dark-haired man, her eyebrow raised.

The dark-haired man with the titanium arm shrugged, then asked, "What happened to the operative?"

The Colonel's eyes bore into him. "He's in the wind. I see you recognize the design."

"Yes," said Pavluk.

"Is there anything you failed to report to J2 and command after your last assignment?" The Colonel waited patiently.

Major Maxwell stepped in. "Alex?"

Alex Pavluk tapped his fingers against the polished wooden surface of the table. His mission to Belarus had been a success. No one suspected the cripple hired on as day labor of contaminating the Druzhba pipeline, the key oil pipeline extending from Russia to Central Europe and Germany. Redirecting the organic chloride vat to over-fill inside the nine-million barrels headed to the west caused exactly the damage hoped for spiking tensions between Russia and Belarus and causing more than $500 million in lost revenue. With the west refusing to pay for contaminated oil and Russia demanding they pay up first before filing a claim, this had the desired effect of weakening the Kremlin who were fast developing new, technologically advanced nuclear weapons. Sabotage complete, he disappeared, coming back to the states via Poland.

"Nothing, sir. I gave a full report and my mission was successfully completed as tasked."

Eastwood listened to the soldier's words. They were the right words, but he didn't like the man's tone of voice. It skirted the edge of respect. It might simply be that this man called Pavluk didn't like having his integrity questioned, but something about it sounded defensive. Whatever it was, it struck a chord in him, one in which the man's first impression failed to impress. Most people never bounced back from that first impression, especially not with Eastwood. In that moment, he hoped he'd never have to spend any time with Pavluk. It wouldn't end well.

The Colonel took a breath before looking at Joely. She returned his gaze, but to Eastwood's eyes, she looked flustered. "I got your assessment," said the Colonel. "We're looking into Riddle. In the meantime, everyone within the inner workings of PATCH-COM will be interviewed over the next week." He turned his attention back to those gathered around the table. "Those of you capable will be dispatched to Kiev. The mission is to locate and interrogate the Kremlin operative. We need to know how he came into possession of an American Special Forces weaponized warrior prosthetic."

"Weaponized warrior?" Eastwood spoke before he could shove the words back down his throat.

The Colonel eyed him. "Yes. Broke-Dick Defense, if you will. Each of you have been chosen for your specialties, Sgt. Tyler. Yes, I know who you are," he said, noting the mild surprise on Eastwood's face. "Your field experience and weapons knowledge are invaluable to this country and we will see a return on our investment in you. Any problem with that?"

"No, sir." Eastwood's reply was automatic, but the gears in his brain began to spin.

"Good," said the Colonel. He looked at Maxwell. "Major, I trust you'll assemble a competent team. They need to be ready to deploy at 0530 in the hangar. No tardiness. No excuses."

"Sir, yes, sir," she said.

The Colonel pushed back from the table and got up. Everyone stood at attention. He nodded, offering a brief salute as he headed out the door.

Major Maxwell got to work. "Holiday, Moreno, Mac, Diaz, Pavluk, and Tyler," she said, looking around the room.

The woman with hostile brown eyes and Pavluk nodded. The quiet man standing next to Major Maxwell stepped forward joining Pavluk and the woman Eastwood now knew was called Moreno. He looked at Ben who came around the table to stand next to him and Diaz.

"The rest of you are dismissed," said Maxwell.

Jackson and Matt turned to leave. Joely gathered her things and followed, throwing a last look over her shoulder at Eastwood.

She looked worried. He offered a half-smile and then turned to his commanding officer tamping down the feeling of unease that snaked through him. It settled like a heavy stone in his gut.

CHAPTER 6

It had been months since he'd had any need to pack an operations bag, but he hadn't forgotten the necessities. Packing was always Eastwood's time of reflection, the moment he organized his thoughts along with his essential items. After the non-essential personnel left the conference room, Major Maxwell informed him and the others chosen that they would all be traveling to Kiev, Ukraine via separate routes and would rendezvous at a central location upon arrival. They'd been given airline tickets, each departing at a different time on a different airline once they completed the first leg of the journey. From Nevada to New York City's Kennedy International, they'd all be together. After that, they'd go nomad. Nothing unusual from anything he'd done before except before he'd been intact. Eastwood had swallowed his misgivings, pushing them down deep as his commander dismissed them.

Now, he was packing his Op bag. T-shirts, a couple of hoodies, a jacket, two pairs of blue jeans, a pair of Khakis, all items in neutral shades to blend in. In addition to clothing he added a small travel compass, a Zebra pen, a waterproof map of Ukraine neatly folded, a couple of handcuff keys, and a mouth guard that he placed into a hard-plastic eyeglass case. An undetectable plastic cuff key was slid into the waistband of the pants he would wear traveling, and his athletic shoes were laced up with Kevlar shoelaces.

The rest of the necessary items for a daily carry kit would have to be purchased when he landed in the Ukraine. The wad of cash in his money clip guaranteed those purchases. He checked his Smart Watch, making sure it had a fresh battery, and added the two burner phones given to him—one to carry and one to place inside his duffel bag. With a few more personal care items and some gauze wrap for his stump, he was ready. Now all he had to do was get through the next ten hours. Anxiety made him pace the room.

Eastwood felt comfortable and confident ambulating around base on his new leg. He'd worked out daily strengthening his body and he'd even begun to jog around the track in the gym. Why, then, did he suddenly feel completely unprepared?

A knock at his door interrupted his pacing.

"Penny for your thoughts?"

Joely stood in the doorway, hands behind her back.

"Depends. How many pennies ya got?" he asked, coming to a stop.

She pulled a face. "No pennies, actually, but I have this?" She brought her hands forward, holding a bottle of whiskey in one and two red Dixie cups in the other.

He chuckled. "What's that for?"

She stepped in, kicking the door closed with her silver heel. "It's for whatever ails you, and you look like maybe a shot or two might be just what you need. What's wrong, Harry?"

Joely set the bottle down on the table at his bedside and unscrewed the cap, pouring out a dram in each cup.

He stepped closer, taking one and knocking back the contents. The whiskey burned as it slid down his throat and warmth spread throughout his body. He exhaled, eyes closed, enjoying the rush. "Damn, that's not bad at all."

"So, are you avoiding the question or just avoiding me?"

He filled his cup again and clinked it against hers in a mock salute. "I'm not avoiding you. Just got a lot on my mind."

Joely sipped her drink. She noticed he'd backed away and that didn't sit well with her ego despite her personal no fraternization policy. Stepping closer, she asked, "And what's going on in that steel trap of yours? Are you having doubts?"

Eastwood looked down into her upturned face. In any other situation a beautiful woman with a Dixie cup of liquor would be a temptation he couldn't resist, but right now, nothing about his current situation felt right. He'd lost more than just his leg in Kuwait. Discovering just how much more of himself he'd lost the night before a mission was not good. Not at all.

"I don't know, Joely. I'm just trying to keep it together. There's no room for doubts."

She didn't like hearing so much uncertainty coming from this big, brave, bold man. "And yet you're having them, aren't you?" she said. Joely laid a manicured hand over his heart. "Your body has healed well. You're strong. Capable. You ran a mile in eight minutes just three days ago in the gym. That's better than average, and I know your titanium leg can withstand a mortar blast. So, what are you doubting, Harry?"

Eastwood tried and then failed to put it into words. This ratcheted up his inner anxiety which in turn pissed him off. "Goddammit, I don't know, Joely. How the hell am I supposed to be feeling going back into the field for the first time since having my goddamned leg blown off, huh? I guess your little program here forgot to focus on that! It's all new. A new leg. New mission. New team. I don't know who I can trust or what!" Eastwood sat down on the side of his bed, his face contorted into a mix of anxiety and frustration, and just a hint of fear.

Joely was dumbfounded. This wasn't Harry. This wasn't the bold Green Beret who'd swooped in and stolen her away from his drunken buddy. This wasn't the man who'd rocked her world all night in a posh London suite. Somewhere along the line in his rehabilitation, Harry had forgotten who the hell he was. But she knew a sure-fire way how to remind him. Time to break her own rule.

She knocked back the whiskey in her cup and slammed the plastic down onto the side table. With careful deliberation, she began unbuttoning her blouse.

Eastwood froze. "What the hell are you doing?"

"Saving your ass," she said, pulling the blouse from her shoulders. She stood in her pale blue slacks and eyelet brassier proudly. She knew her cups literally "runneth over" and there was no shame in her game. Without hesitation, she reached behind her back and unsnapped the bra letting it slide down and fall to the floor.

Eastwood exhaled. It sounded exactly like someone punched him in the gut.

"These tits are made in the U.S. of A, Harold Tyler. These are what you're fighting for. This one's Liberty," she said, lifting the left breast, "and this one's Justice," she added, lifting the right.

Swallowing hard, Eastwood stared like a schoolboy, mouth agape.

Joely began unbuttoning her pants and with a sexy wiggle, shimmied them down her long legs and then one at a time, removed them from each foot. Like a seasoned stripper, she mic-dropped them next to her bra. Now wearing only her white thong panties and silver heels, she slid her hands down her body until her fingers formed a vee over her mons. "And this, darlin', is Freedom."

"You're crazy, woman," he said, glancing up and catching her watching him intently.

"Yeah? What are you going to do about it, Harry?" She closed the space between them. With one hand on his chest, she pushed him back and climbed onto the bed straddling his hips.

There was a shift in Eastwood's green eyes. Hunger roared to life and desire shot through him reminding him he still had functioning appendages. He gripped her hips, squeezing her ass and growled, "I'm gonna pleasure you until you're screaming my name, just like London."

"I don't know," she said, playing coy. "Are you sure you're up to it? Up to these," she asked, cupping her breasts.

His eyes riveted on her rosy nipples. "Liberty and Justice are all mine, baby, and then I'm going to dive hard into Freedom." He thrust his hips and added, "really hard!"

Heat suffused her body. Joely began this seduction to boost his confidence, but now she was so hot, so wet, she could hardly stand it.

"Then fuck me, baby. Show me how a badass soldier pleasures a woman!" She yanked her panties off and then reached for his zipper. He was already on it, unbuttoning, unzipping, and pushing his pants down over his hips.

Joely reached inside his underwear and wrapped her hand around his thick shaft, freeing it from confinement.

His face contorted in exquisite pain, but he groaned his pleasure, sucking air through his teeth. "Sweet baby Jesus!"

"Preach to me, baby," she said, and then with a practiced motion, raised up and came down on his stiff member, taking it all in. "Oh, God, yes! Damn, Harry, I forgot how good you feel." She began to ride him.

Eastwood held on like a rookie rodeo cowboy trying to last eight seconds. With each thrust of her sweet hips, her beautiful, full breasts bounced and swayed. He fumbled, hitting the button on the hospital bed to raise his head. Slowly, he eliminated the distance between his mouth and her nipples. Finally, he clamped down on Liberty and gave Justice a friendly squeeze. Joely moaned.

"Oh, yes. Bite my nipples. You know I like that."

He did as bid, letting her take her pleasure. He was so painfully hard he didn't know how much longer he'd last.

She seemed to sense this and was thankfully on the same page. Gripping his ears, she held his face between her breasts and thrust harder. "Tell me you love my tits!"

"I love your titties! Dear God, I love titties," he said, his voice muffled.

"And you love freedom!" She threw in a wicked wiggle with her next thrust.

"Fuck yeah, I love freedom!" Sweat beaded on his brow as both their bodies grew slick.

"And you're a badass Green Beret," she panted, thrusting harder. "No one can ever take that away from you. Do it for me. Do it for Liberty! Do it for Justice! Do it for Freeeeeeeedommmmmmm!" she sang, climaxing.

Hearing her come, Eastwood lost it. He pumped hard once, twice, three times more. Then, he threw back his head and howled like a wolf.

They slumped together, each panting, trying to catch their breath.

Eastwood recovered first, reaching up to caress a strand of her blonde hair that came loose from her updo. It was in the afterglow that he realized he hadn't even kissed her. He wanted to now. Lifting her chin, he gently took her lips in a soft kiss.

"Thank you," he said, his voice gruff with emotion.

"For what," she whispered, enjoying the tickle of his beard.

"For reminding me I'm still a man."

Joely grinned. "Damn right, you are. Still having any doubts?"

"None," he answered. "You having any regrets?"

She kissed him, long and slow. Breathless again, she pulled back. "None."

"Good," he said, "because we've still got a few hours to kill before lights' out and I think I need a little more remindin'."

CHAPTER 7

J oely watched as the newly assembled team of Eastwood, Holiday, Moreno, Mac, Diaz, and Pavluk loaded up in the transport truck. Harry peeked out at her throwing a quick wink. Then the cheeky devil blew a kiss. Alex Pavluk caught the move out of the corner of his eye and turned to see Joely blushing. She quickly looked at each of the team in turn, keeping out of the way as Major Maxwell went over the plans one last time.

She didn't know why she felt the need to be there at 0530, but there she stood. After their night of hot lovemaking, she'd slipped out of Harry's room returning to her own. She'd hardly slept. All she could think about was what they'd done. She didn't regret any of it. She knew Harry's confidence was restored. He'd proven that several times to her immense delight, but she did worry about their working relationship. It would be bad if it got out they were fucking. Worse if anyone realized she had feelings for Sgt. Tyler. That was the thing that surprised her most. When she dug deep enough, she knew it wasn't simply a professional need to boost his confidence before a mission. She'd missed him.

Special Operator Eastwood had impressed the hell out of her in London. For such a big man, he was surprisingly gentle, and a superb lover. More so, he was smart and funny, and he lived life the way she did. Without apology. For months now they'd been dancing around each other. She tried to maintain distance while he was having none of it. It was like foreplay and when they'd finally come together last night, it was a tantric explosion. The orgasms were fierce, each one better than the last. And damn, he was such a good kisser!

When Joely finally slept, it was with a smile on her lips. She dreamt of Harry chasing her. Dreamed he made love to her again in a field of cotton candy and Skittles. Then, he was gone. She could hear him calling her name, fear and desperation in his voice, but she couldn't see him. Instead, there was someone else, a dark form whose face she couldn't quite make out stalking her. She awoke panicked at 0445. Quickly, she'd showered and thrown on some clothes making it to the transport bay just in time to see her man off. *Her man? When did that happen?*

Professionalism came first so she kept to the back of the bay. But when Harry winked at her and puckered his lips, her body responded, and her heart leapt with joy. Her worry ratcheted up several notches when the engine started, and the truck moved toward the tunnel leading out. Her heart was on that truck. Watching it drive away hurt like hell.

Major Maxwell approached, her limp more pronounced today. "You're up early."

Joely nodded. "Wasn't sure if anyone needed anything before heading out. Thought I'd make myself available just in case."

Sydelle Maxwell eyed Joely. The sharp woman never missed a thing. It was her special skill along with her indomitable will. "I see. Is that a hickey?" She pointed at Joely's neck and with a chuckle, left the bay.

"Damn," Joely muttered, yanking up the collar of her blouse. Quickly, she returned to her room.

⁂

The truck rumbled up the long and winding ramp out of Camp Lazarus finally emerging above-ground. Dark skies on the edge of dawn greeted his eyes. It was the first time

Eastwood had been on the surface since arriving at base camp. He, Diaz, and Holiday quietly enjoyed this moment. Pavluk, the one called Mac, and Moreno didn't seem to notice, giving away the fact that they'd been outside recently, and to them, this wasn't a big deal.

It didn't take a genius to understand those three had been at base camp for some time, having gone through their rehabilitation long before he had. It was also obvious this wasn't their first time back in the field. He knew that for sure about Pavluk after their meeting yesterday. In answering the Colonel's question, he'd revealed a recent mission. A successful one at that. It didn't change the fact that Eastwood disliked the man, but it did earn a grudging respect. When it came to missions, soldiers supported each other regardless of personal feelings. He needed to keep that in mind. Other than the strange impression he'd given during their briefing, Eastwood knew he had no real reason to dislike the man. He decided he would strive to keep an open mind.

With that, he let his thoughts drift to last night. It was all he could do to squelch the smile from overtaking his face. He didn't want to give anything away to his teammates. His relationship with Joely was none of their business and it existed before he'd been brought to Camp Lazarus. He didn't feel the least bit bad about it either. Joely was a special woman. Smart as a whip. Funny on a sarcastic level he could well-appreciate, and sexy as all get-out. The woman had it all. Plus, she fucked like a champion. He'd never known anyone like her. Still, he didn't know how he could fit into her world.

She was a successful businesswoman, a goddamned science prodigy at that, while he was just a soldier. Low man on the totem pole. His purpose was to follow orders. Hers was to give them. She'd given him plenty of orders last night, and he'd gratefully obliged. The smile he fought snuck halfway across his lips. Bite this, lick that. Go harder. Go faster. Kiss me. Bite me again. Spank my ass. Damn! He could really fall for a woman like Joely Winter.

"What're you so happy about, Eastwood?"

Art Diaz watched him, an amused look on his face.

"Just happy to be outside, man. And you? You worried about any of this?"

Art shook his head. "Naw. My eyesight is better than it's ever been. I think once we're there, it'll be just like riding a bike."

"Yeah," said Ben. "Just need to stay the course. Find the operative. Do our thing."

"It's not quite that easy, Holiday," said Pavluk, butting in.

"Sure it is," said Moreno. She glared at Alex Pavluk. "If you find it difficult, maybe this isn't your line of work."

Eastwood liked the hostile woman already. He extended his hand. "Harold Tyler. You can call me Eastwood."

She shook his hand, her grip firm. "Like Dirty Harry. I get it. Nastjia Moreno. Call me Nasty."

"This is Art Diaz," he said, making the introductions, "and Ben Holiday. He's our medic."

"Fucking Doc Holiday. No shit?" she said.

"No shit, ma'am," Holiday replied.

The smile slipped from Nasty's lips. "Don't call me ma'am or I'll have to rearrange your testicles."

"Oh, shit!" Diaz laughed. "Ben, my friend, you've met your match."

Ben smiled, unfazed by Nastjia's threat. "Looks that way. My apologies—"

"Don't say it," she warned.

"Nasty," he replied, honey dripping from his lips.

Her eyes narrowed.

At the back of the truck, Mac shook his head.

"That's Mac. Gerry Maclean. He isn't sociable, but he's good people, as long as you don't cross him," said Nasty.

Her words were dire, but there was genuine affection in her tone. "And you know this one from the meeting yesterday. Alex Pavluk."

Alex glanced around the interior but remained standoff-ish.

"Don't mind him," she said to the men. "He can't help it."

"Brain damage," asked Art.

"Naw, he's just an asshole," she replied.

Eastwood bit his lip to keep from laughing. He knew now without a doubt he liked Moreno. And her spot-on assessment of Pavluk confirmed his own misgivings. It wasn't just him. Apparently, he'd struck the same wrong nerve with Nasty.

"Shut your hole, Petty Officer Moreno." Pavluk muttered.

"So formal," said Ben. "What's that all about?"

From the back of the truck, Mac muttered. "He's not allowed to call her Nasty."

The men were surprised. First, to hear the quiet, formidable Mac speak, and second, by his revelation.

"And why not?" asked Eastwood. Somehow, he knew it was going to be good.

Mac pinned him with a dark glare. "He's the reason she got the nickname. As punishment, she doesn't let him use it. When he tried—"

"I put him on his ass," she finished Mac's sentence. Throwing a lethal look at Pavluk, she glowered. "And if he does it again, he knows I'm going to kill him."

Pavluk flipped her off, but kept his mouth closed.

Eastwood, Ben, and Art sat, mouths agog. Their respect for Petty Officer Natsjia "Nasty' Moreno grew ten-fold. She might be small in stature, but she had big balls.

"I'd really like to hear that story sometime, Nasty," said Eastwood, enjoying the dig at Pavluk.

She smirked. "We got some time coming up, Eastwood. Buy me a drink on the plane and I'll tell you all about it."

"Deal," he grinned.

For the first time, Eastwood looked forward to the journey.

CHAPTER 8

The flight to JFK International revealed a host of information. Over tiny bottles of vodka mixed with equally tiny cans of orange juice, Petty Officer Moreno told Eastwood her story. She was the first woman to pass SEAL training, but during her first mission, the swell of the ocean pushed her into the propeller end of the inflatable boat she was boarding with her team. They were rendezvousing with the U.S.S. John McCain in the Gulf of Aden having fled quickly from a small village on the Somali coast. As she tried to hoist herself into the craft, the wave pushed her legs into the propeller. Her left foot got caught. Her team members killed the engine and pulled her in, but by the time they reached the McCain, the damage was done, and so was her career as the first female SEAL.

With no family to go home to, she'd accepted the offer to be a guinea pig for the military's new program, PATCH-COM.

"What happened to your family?"

She knocked back the last of her drink and sighed. "My mom died ten years ago in a car accident. Police report says the car was found off the 556 near the Cibola National Forest. Ran right off the road into a gulley. Never understood that. We lived in West Mesa in Albuquerque. There was no reason for her to be up in that direction. She worked in West Mesa. Papa said he tried to get police to investigate, but as far as they were concerned, a Russian immigrant dying in a car accident wasn't worth their time."

"Russian?" Eastwood's ears perked.

"Yeah. Nadia was from the Baltic region of Russia. She came here as a teenager with my grandmother. Was working her way through the citizenship process when she met my dad. They fell in love even though they had a difficult time communicating at first. She spoke very little English. Same with my dad. He was a day laborer as a young man, but he worked hard and became the manager at our local slaughterhouse. They both worked their asses off trying to pay bills and still be able to keep up with the payments for their green cards and all the fees to become citizens. That shit is expensive, you know? It's no wonder so many people are still undocumented that come to the U.S."

"So, you speak Russian and Spanish I take it?"

"Da and Si," she chuckled.

"Where's your dad now?"

She shrugged. "I don't know. For a few years he hung around trying to make it work, make sure I graduated high school, but after I joined the Navy, he disappeared. I mean, I think he just couldn't take it anymore, about my mom. He was so broken-hearted. Her death changed him. He went from being happy to an empty shell. I tried to find him. I don't think he's in America anymore. I think he went back to Mexico City. I've got some relatives there. An uncle and aunt. Some cousins I've never met. But he left. Didn't say goodbye or leave a note. Just up and went, and I haven't seen him since." She turned away, looking out the window.

Eastwood's respect for Moreno cemented. She'd gone through some heavy shit, mostly alone. A lot of people would've given up, but she didn't. She'd moved forward and successfully completed training in one of the world's elite special forces groups. That was hard enough for a man. Most men didn't make it through, but for a woman to earn her place in the best of the best was something. To do it without anyone cheering her on was amazing. He looked to his right at Ben and Art. Both men had listened quietly while she shared her story. Humbled, they ordered another round of drinks.

Ben handed her another airplane screwdriver. "Respect, Moreno. Now, get to the juicy bits. What'd Pavluk do to piss you off?"

She took the drink and clinked each of the plastic cups. She threw a mean glare at the back of Alex's head. He sat two rows up next to the aisle away from the rest. Mac was one row up in front of Diaz squashed between a large woman and a man busy tapping away on his computer. He looked as angry as she felt. "I don't want to talk about that. Suffice to say he picked the wrong woman to fuck with."

Eastwood listened more to the subtleties in her tone than her words. It was something he'd always been good at; reading between the lines. He picked up on the little things like body language, timing, what a person said, and what they didn't say. All those things added up to something bad. He sensed it. Alex Pavluk had done a number on Moreno, and with the rampant sexual abuse in the military, it wasn't hard to figure out that he'd either attempted to harm her or he succeeded. Then he remembered Mac's words. That Moreno had put Pavluk on his ass for calling her Nasty. Math always added up and if he had to make a wager, he'd bet Pavluk tried to have his way with the hot-headed Nastjia, and when she refused his advances, he harassed her verbally. That would be when she put an end to that violently once and for all. And she still had to work with him.

He shook his head. He'd wanted to be open-minded, but any man who hurts a woman is a piece of shit in his book. His first impression of Pavluk had been that the man was an arrogant asshole. Now he was sure of it. Eastwood felt instantly protective of his new teammate. He decided then and there he'd do everything he could to keep Alex Pavluk from getting anywhere near Nastjia. The looks on Ben's and Art's faces told him they would do the same. They knew more about her now, but a question about another still nagged.

"What's Mac's story? What's his disability?"

Nastjia shrugged. "Nothing physical. He is," she paused. "He *was* an Army Airborne Ranger. Long and decorated career, but he saw too much, I think. He won't talk about it, not to any of us. Wasn't even supposed to be at PATCH."

This surprised him. "Then how'd he come to be there?"

"Just another government paperwork screw-up. Maxwell grew kinda fond of him I think while they tried to sort out the mess. Decided to keep him. Mac didn't want to go anyhow. He doesn't have any close family. PTSD is his issue, but he keeps a lid on it mostly. Staying at base camp seems to help. That's why he's none too friendly. Usually scares the crap out of most people. They say he gives off a weird vibe, but he's always been kind to me. After I put Pavluk on his ass, Mac stepped in ready to tear him a new one." She smiled, lost for a moment in the memory. "I told him that wouldn't be necessary. I fight my own battles."

Eastwood absorbed her words. His view of Mac altered, growing more positive. Learning more about his new team was important. He needed to know he could count on these men...and woman. The jury was out on Pavluk. He knew he didn't like the man, but whether he could count on him in battle was a separate issue altogether. As for the rest, he felt reasonably comfortable.

Bonded now over shared stories and cheap vodka, they settled in for the remainder of their flight. In two hours, they would be landing at JFK. From there, each would be going their separate ways, ultimately reuniting at a hostel on the east side of the Kiev. No one paid attention to travelers in hostels which was exactly how they needed it to be. Going nomad meant anonymity. They operated in the dark, beneath the radar, and off the grid. They would formulate a plan and find the Ukrainian operative, interrogate him, get the information they needed, and hand him off to the CIA. Then, he'd come back home to Joely, see if he could convince her to break a few more rules.

CHAPTER 9

After twenty-five hours of nonstop travel, Eastwood finally arrived in Kiev. Having gone their separate ways at JFK, he was the first to arrive. Ben and Art were due in five hours coming from different directions, and Nasty was to arrive in three. Pavluk and Mac were due shortly after Ben and Art. All were to meet up at the nearest hostel to Borispol International Airport. A short cab ride delivered him to the West End Hostel, Kiev. The room he was shown to barely qualified as livable. Even the shittiest American hotels beat this boarding house. There were two twin beds against either wall with a small bedside table in between. Walking space between the beds was about two feet. The carpet reeked of mold and age and thousands of pairs of dirty feet trafficking across it over the years. What was probably once crisp white paint on the walls was now a faded yellow. Cigarette smoke, air pollution, and time did a lot of damage.

He picked the bed on the far wall setting his bag down. He'd paid double to ensure no one else would be booked into the room with him. This guaranteed privacy and if the hostel booked up quickly, would provide at least one of the team a place to sleep. He had three hours to kill before Nastjia arrived. Pulling out his map of the city, he pinpointed his current position and then located the hotel where the stolen plans had been found. He would recon the hotel, see what information he could gather. With any luck, there were security cameras either in or around the hotel. It was the surest way to begin tracking the agent who'd been in possession of the schematics. He assumed it was an agent, but it could easily be a lower level operative hoping to capitalize on the tech outlined in the renderings of one of Joely's designs. It could also be a gopher, someone tasked with delivering from person A to person B. Either way, it was the place to start.

Eastwood pulled out his carry-all, a leather cross-body bag. Inside, he carried a few items such as cigarettes, a lighter, a compass, floss, a cuff key hidden inside a fake tube of lip balm, and some cash. There were a few other items he needed to procure, and that meant finding a local market. According to the map, there was one such on the way to the hotel. He'd pick up what he needed there. His plan made, he slid his duffel bag under the bed, and heading out, made sure to lock the door. Across the hall, a DO NOT DISTURB sign hung on a doorknob. He lifted it, hanging it on his own door to deter any maids, if the dirty hostel even had any. He was none too sure, but someone had to provide the towels and such. It was a subtle extra layer of security on his tiny room. Anyone passing by would think the room occupied. He pulled a knit cap out of his jacket pocket, and yanking it down over his hair, walked quickly through the miniscule lobby and out the door. When he hit the street, he turned left making his way five blocks down Zakhidna Street to the open market.

He passed an old cemetery along the way. The bronze of the sign had long since turned green, but it read 'Shulyavs'ke Cemetery.' The tall trees cast gloomy shadows over the massive graveyard. The weeds had overgrown the grounds. The cemetery was dotted with graves enclosed within rusted-out wrought-iron fences. He never understood the need to fence in the dead. They weren't going anywhere, were they? The entire place gave him the willies. He yanked the collar of his jacket up around his neck. A sudden chill wind whistled past his ears as Eastwood picked up the pace wanting to leave the old burial ground behind him as quickly as possible.

Plant debris clogged the gutters of the street and the scents of wet earth and decay filled his nose. He was a long way from home, he knew, but it felt more like a different era than a different location. His thoughts kept him occupied while he put one foot in front of the other. When he reached the market, he felt a bit better. People wandered around shopping. The sounds of their voices were an added comfort. He weaved his way through locating what he needed, and in reasonably passing Russian, made his purchases. He didn't speak Ukrainian, but thankfully, the languages were similar, and many Ukrainian citizens spoke or understood Russian. As he packed his items inside his carry-all, he passed a small kiosk selling tourist trinkets. One rack contained postcards. He picked one up. The picture on the front was a panoramic view of downtown Kiev. The back was blank. He paid the seller and added the postcard to his bag. With a smile, he thought of Joely. Under better circumstances, he knew she would love wandering the open-air market. She'd admitted her love of shopping back in London when he'd seen the crazy amount of luggage she brought to their wild weekend-turned-crazy-kidnapping.

Had her best friend, Emma, not been taken by a terrorist, he was sure she would've bought out the stores including another suitcase or two to carry the items back to the states.

Delicious scents tickled his nose. A food vendor near the market's entry was selling Varenyky. Americans knew them as pierogi. The aroma drew him in, not having eaten since dinner the night before. He purchased a plate along with a bottled water. The warm dumplings were filled with sauerkraut and mashed potatoes. He downed ten of them as he made his way to Mashynobudyvna Street. There, he hung another left. It was another two miles to reach the Inn Kiev. When he arrived, he walked the perimeter searching for security cameras pointed toward the Inn's front doors and the back entry. There were two street cameras, but they would do him no good. There was no way he'd get access to the city's traffic cameras, but luck shined upon him. A small shop located across the street had a security camera facing out. It was a legal services office, one that closed at four in the afternoon.

He went around back looking for a secondary entrance. There, next to a garbage container shared by the row of businesses was a door. There was a camera in the back as well pointed at that door. If he approached from the side, he could disable it. The lock on the door was a simple tumbler. No deadbolt which made his plan easier. When the staff left for the night and locked up, he and the team could break in, find the security monitors inside, and with luck, locate a tape from the time period before the CIA agents found the plans in the hotel room across the street. If fortune shined upon them, they'd be able to discover who rented the room before then. All they had was the room number—room 210—and a date range within three days of discovery. According to the hotel map he'd pulled up online, room 210 faced out to the street.

Eastwood had his work cut out for him. He looked at his watch. Nastjia would be arriving soon. He headed across the street to the hotel. If he couldn't get to the registry, he would need the next best informant, housekeeping. He wasn't above bribing some poor maid for information. The skies above grew cloudy and the temperature began to drop. His leg ached, phantom pains mostly. He still had them, but some of the pain came from his stump. Despite all the rehab, this was the most sustained physical exertion he'd undergone since losing his lower left leg. He blamed both the lengthy travel, exhaustion, and the chilly winds of Kiev. The sooner he gathered the intel, the sooner he could return to the hostel and rest. He would need it for the coming night. Breaking and entering was hard work. More so when it was being done by a bunch of broke dick soldiers. Sucking it up, he made his way across the street disappearing through the front doors.

*　*　*

Nastjia was in the lobby when he arrived back at the hostel. She'd donned a wig, a short blonde bob, but he recognized the attitude in her stance. She was popping gum impatiently while the clerk finished checking her in. He waited near the lift. After receiving her key, she joined him. He noticed only the slightest limp from her prosthetic foot. To the casual observer, it didn't register, but he knew. They waited until the doors closed and the elevator began ascending before speaking.

"Been out on recon already?" she asked.

"I did." Eastwood leaned onto his right leg easing the pressure on the left.

"Find anything?"

"A business across from the Inn Kiev has a security camera that faces the front of the hotel. Easy access through the back. They close at four. We can break in after dark without any trouble. I didn't see any alarm system wires near the back door."

She shifted her duffel bag to her right shoulder as the doors slid open. "You on this floor too?"

"Yeah. Down on the left," he said, pointing.

She glanced at her key. "Looks like I'm over here," she said, looking right. "Anything else?"

"I sweet-talked a maid at the hotel. She's been there for the past six months. Told her my cousin stayed there a month back, stayed in room 210. Gave her the date. She says she remembers a man in that room at that time, but he stayed only two of the three days he paid for, that someone else took over the room because my cousin left early. I think that was the CIA. Sounds like this guy knew he was being trailed, which would explain why he bugged out in such a hurry that he left those plans behind. But what gets me is, why would he leave them?"

Nasty inserted her key card, thinking. "Maybe they weren't the reason he was there."

Eastwood cocked his head. "You think the plans were an extra? Something outside this agent's main mission?"

"It's the only thing that would make sense. He might not have realized what he had."

He pondered that for a moment. "But who gave them to him, that's what we need to find out."

"That's why we're here."

"Goddamned CIA slips us only the tip of the information they have. Doesn't bother to tell us why they were trailing this guy to begin with."

"And we get shafted," she said. "How much time do we have before the others arrive?" She threw her duffel bag inside on the bed. She'd managed to grab a single. No one else would share her room.

"Two hours for Ben and Art. Jerkwad and Mac arrive after them."

"Jerkwad?"

Eastwood chuckled. "Pavluk's new name. Don't tell him."

"As if I'd waste my breath. I guess I can hold out another couple hours. We'll eat when they arrive, then make our plans."

"Sounds good. You got everything," he asked, peeking into her small room. Hers had its own bathroom, tiny though it was.

"Yeah. I'm good. Just gonna get settled and rest a bit."

"Rest sounds good. Can't believe I said that. Shit, gettin' old."

Nasty noticed he was favoring his good leg. "Naw, you're just still healing. It takes time, Dirty Harry. Believe me. I was in the same position last year. You'll get there, old man," she smirked. "Go rest and then come knock when you're ready to meet up with the group."

Eastwood nodded. "Thanks, Natjia." He appreciated her sharing that information. It was good to know, especially now when he was in pain. Having someone around who understood made a world of difference to his flagging self-esteem.

He limped off to his room. Once inside, he was grateful for the crappy twin bed. Grabbing the pillow from the opposite bed, he settled down, removing his prosthetic. He propped it up against the nightstand and then shoved the extra pillow beneath his leg, lying back. The relief was instant. Reaching down to the floor, he rummaged around inside his bag for the tube of salve he'd brought along. The steroidal anti-inflammatory worked quickly once rubbed in. A sigh escaped his lips as he got comfortable. Within moments, he was sound asleep.

CHAPTER 10

"So, you're taking point without a vote from the rest of the team?" Alex Pavluk eyed Eastwood over a pint of beer.

"I was the first to arrive. First to arrive recons for the team. If you don't want to do a B & E, just say so, but you'll be wasting everyone's time if you insist on your plan. We can ID the occupant on our own."

The tension between the two men was thick. As soon as he'd arrived, Alex made a power-grab giving orders for the team to recon the neighborhood around the Inn Kiev and to find a way into the hotel's offices. He wanted to hack into their computer system and find out the name of the occu-pant of room 210 on the date one month previous. This would work if they had more time but breaking into a busy hotel undetected would be difficult and require planning. Breaking into the office across the street after hours held more promise.

And Eastwood was having none of Alex's crap. As a senior Special Operations Weapons Specialist, he had the most experience and higher rank than Pavluk. Pavluk argued he'd been a PATCH longer, familiar with how the unit operated. The situation was like two mountain goats butting horns.

Mac, who rarely spoke, smacked his hand down on the table startling everyone.

"We don't have time for this bullshit." He looked at Pavluk. "Whether you like it or not, Sgt. Tyler is right. We don't have time to do a second reconnaissance and we definitely don't have time to find a way to hack into the hotel's computer system. All we need is a face on film and we can get an ID through command's facial recognition. I'm in, Sergeant," he said, addressing Eastwood.

"Me too," said Ben.

Art nodded, lifting his mug before taking a sip of the warm beer. He made a face. "Sooner we get an ID, the faster I can get back to cold brews.

Nastjia snorted. "Amen.

Alex fumed, but said nothing. He sipped his beer. "Alright, Sergeant, we'll do it your way."

"What time do you want to head out, Harry," asked Nastjia.

Eastwood answered, but shot a look at Pavluk. "Nine, Nasty. It takes a good thirty minutes to walk there and any cleaning crew should've come and gone by then. Art, you'll be the lookout. We don't need any local police rolling up on us. Ben, Nasty, help Art keep us under the radar. Mac, Alex, you're coming in with me. The lock is simple," he began, outlining the plan. Pen in hand, Eastwood sketched out a map of the area on a cocktail napkin.

By the time their food arrived, the plan was made. At the end of the meal, they'd talked through it twice. When they were finished, Mac and Alex headed out to a local hardware store for the necessary items. Ben and Art were told to rest up for the night, and Eastwood and Nasty grabbed a taxi heading over to the Inn to clock police and security sweeps around the building opposite the hotel. It would help their plan to know when and how often the buildings were monitored.

In the hour before the legal services office closed, there was no sign of police in the area. There were also no security officers, either by vehicle or on foot patrol. Once the office closed, things changed. Eastwood and Nasty watched two suited-up lawyer types exit the front of the building. One locked the front door and took off on foot towards the subway station. The other, a short man, walked around back, carrying a briefcase. A few minutes later, a gray Renault Laguna emerged pulling into traffic and driving off. The lights inside the office were out, the CLOSED sign showing prominently through the small, street-side window. By five o'clock, a police unit rolled down the street, and turning into the side street, made a pass down the back alley. The unit didn't return again until ten past six. Eastwood and Nasty figured on hourly passes which meant when they arrived at 9:30, they would have less than thirty minutes to break in, find what they needed, and get out before getting caught.

He looked at his teammate. "We might need to leave the hostel twenty minutes earlier. Give ourselves a little more time. We'd arrive just after the nine o'clock sweep."

"Makes sense. It'll give you guys more time to locate the CCTV tapes. Hopefully, they have the dates logged and backed up onto their server."

"It's a legal service. I'm betting good money it's not only backed up, but efficiently labeled."

"Yeah. If not, they're shitty lawyers. Ready to head back?"

"Ready."

They walked to the front of the hotel and procured a taxi that had just dropped off a new guest. The driver was reluctant saying he needed to get back to the airport, but when Eastwood gave him the name of the hostel, he shrugged knowing it was on the way. He wouldn't lose time and gained another fare on the return trip.

In less than three hours, it would be Go-time.

The team took off in pairs. Eastwood and Nasty left first. Five minutes afterwards, Ben and Art took off, and behind them, Mac and Alex left. It was important not to draw attention to themselves as a group. To this end, they split up, not publicly acknowledging each other inside the hostel. Their late lunch was the only instance they sat together, and even then; each had arrived at different times before commandeering two tables at the back of the pub. It was full of people, locals and tourists alike. The likelihood of drawing attention was low.

Not coming from special operations originally, Art asked, "Why don't we just take the subway or a bus? Why walk?"

Pavluk rolled his eyes and answered, "Because public transportation is monitored by CCTV around the city. Unless we steal a car, we're walking or maybe taking a cab, but we can't order three cabs. It would draw attention. Think before you ask, Art."

Eastwood glared at Pavluk and patted Art's shoulder. "Nomads always operate off the radar, Art. As far as our government is concerned, we're not officially here, as you know. The more we stay hidden, the better."

"Nomads?"

Eastwood shrugged. "That's what we call ourselves in special forces. Violent nomads. Sometimes, we do things that are against the law. Swiftly. Violently. Against our personal conscience. It's called survival. You'll learn. Just remember, there are no dumb questions. Only assholes giving snippy answers," he said, throwing side-eye at Pavluk. "Anything you want to know, just ask me."

"Or me," Nasty added.

Enmity glowed in Pavluk's dark eyes. The look he pinned Eastwood with said he clearly did not like the dirty-blond, red-bearded Green Beret. The amusement in Eastwood's green eyes said he didn't give a fuck.

The incident was the reason Art and Ben put themselves between Eastwood and Pavluk as their teams made their way along the route to the Inn Kiev and the empty legal services office across the street. No matter personal relationships, the team and the mission came first. All other issues had to be put aside. To that end, everyone worked together. Dressed in unassuming drab colors with dark knit caps on their heads, they blended into the night. Temperatures dropped by over twenty degrees after the sun set. A chilly thirty-seven degrees kept them moving quickly to generate heat. With low cloud cover and little light, the only giveaway to their presence moving along Zakhidna Street were puffs of hot breath on the cold air. But few were out, and those that were paid no attention.

Two by two they arrived at the deserted legal services office. Eastwood and Nasty had already ducked down the side street and disabled the security camera at the back door by the time Ben and Art arrived. They fanned out, taking opposite sides as lookouts. Blending into the shadows, they turned on their two-way radios. Mac and Pavluk arrived last, ducking down the side and joining Eastwood and Nasty.

Mac quickly went to work. He dropped down to his knees and pulled out a hand towel unrolling it on the ground. Inside were various tools. Slender screwdrivers in flathead and Phillips head along with smaller versions used to repair eyeglasses were contained within the roll. He looked at the lock and selected what he needed. It was eleven past nine. They had less than forty-nine minutes to get in, find the security tape, and get back out undetected.

Eastwood and Pavluk stood against the wall. Mac worked quietly and quickly. Within two minutes, he'd popped the lock. They were in.

The interior of the office was small. There was the back-room where they entered, two tiny offices with overstuffed bookshelves, and a miniscule lobby. The room at the back, however, was the one they needed. A computer monitor showed current street views of the front of the building. The camera outside the back door showed only static.

"Mac, look through that file cabinet. Pavluk, see if you can hack into their system. I'll check this file cabinet." Eastwood gave the orders.

Each began searching. While Mac and Eastwood went through the drawers methodically, Alex Pavluk tapped the keys with his one good hand to wake up the computer. Oddly enough, it was not passcode protected, but the archived files were not in plain view. It took a bit of hunting to locate the file. It was under 'SecFileRetain.' The language barrier caused the most delay in locating it. Alex found the date they were looking for and pulled up the footage. He hit play, watching for a few minutes. People entered and exited the Inn Kiev. He pulled out a flash drive and inserted it. As he was about to download the file, he noticed a black Audi pull up to the hotel on the video. Two men got out. G-men. Government men always looked like government men. The way they surveilled their surroundings and then entered a building gave them away to keen observers. He'd bet good money these were the CIA agents. After they went through the front doors, another man stepped out from behind one of the front entry pillars. He was a man of medium height, mid-forties, and a balding pate. He wore glasses, a suit in an indistinguishable dark shade, and carried a cross-body bag. He watched the two G-men enter, and then, turned around, walking, then running down the street out of frame.

"I think I've got him," he said.

Eastwood and Mac stopped their own searches and came up behind Pavluk. He rewound the tape and let it play.

"That's our guy," said Eastwood. "Download it and let's get out. We can review the whole tape at the hostel."

"Wait," said Alex. "Now that we know what he looks like, we should get the footage from the two previous days. We can see who he met."

"True," said Mac. "We got enough room on that drive?"

"Yeah," said Alex. "It'll just take a few minutes longer."

Eastwood looked at his watch. "We only have fifteen minutes. That enough time?"

"Should be. Depends on their internet speed." He hit the button and the download began.

The first date went quickly, but during download of day two, the internet stalled. Pavluk drummed his fingers on the desk. "Come on, you dick!"

Eastwood glanced at his watch. "We're cutting it close."

"It'll go. Just wait." Alex hit ENTER again in a vain attempt to force the computer to move faster. It didn't help. Another four minutes passed. Finally, it moved. Day two downloaded. One day left. Pavluk typed in the date and clicked download. It began, but stalled, moving slowly. "Fucking slow-assed Ukrainian internet."

"Come on, man. We're going to have company in five minutes."

"It's going. Just wait." The green line moved again. Eighty-seven percent downloaded. Ninety-two percent downloaded. Ninety-eight percent downloaded. One hundred percent.

"Finally. Get that flash drive out and leave no trace we were here." Eastwood and Mac backed up, moving toward the back door. "Move it, Pavluk."

Alex wiped down the keyboard and pushed the chair back where he found it. They left quickly, locking the door behind them and taking off to the right. Eastwood pulled out his two-way. "Team on the move. Rendezvous back at the hostel. Six out."

Ben and Art moved off separately in the shadows meeting halfway down the street. Pavluk and Mac moved past Eastwood and Nastjia going out to the street from behind the building next door to the legal service.

As Eastwood and Nasty came out to the front of the building, they merged with a group of tourists making their way back to the hotel. The headlights of a passing police cruiser headed their way. By the time the car made it around to the back alley, they were gone.

Across the way, a man took one last draw off a cigarette. He blew out smoke as he flicked it away, stepping off the curb. He made his way quickly to the other side of the street, and with his hands shoved into his pockets, followed the man and woman who'd blended into the crowd of tourists.

CHAPTER 11

Eastwood's room was crowded. Each of the six team members had a spot. Eastwood and Nasty sat on his bed. Art, Ben, and Mac sat on the opposite bed, and Alex sat on the floor between them, allowing more room to stretch out his left leg prosthetic. He supported the laptop on his titanium arm and with his right hand, inserted the flash drive. He pulled up the section of video showing the CIA agents and then the balding man wearing glasses carrying a cross-body bag. He paused the video and showed the man to the group.

"This is who we're looking for on the other tapes. I'll download a date each to your laptops," he said, looking at Art and then Eastwood. "If we split up the three days, we can scan them faster. I'll make a crop of their faces now and send those on to command. They can run 'em through facial recognition."

"Why send the CIA agents' faces?" Art asked.

Pavluk rolled his eyes, opening his mouth to answer. Eastwood cut him off. "Because we need to make sure, and because I for one am curious as to who these agents are and why they aren't following up on their own mess."

"It does seem strange that they sent us in to track this guy down. They could've handled this on their own. Why send special ops?" Nastjia asked.

"The question isn't why send special ops," said Mac. Everyone looked at the quiet man. He grunted, his deep-set eyes ever hostile. "The question is why send in the short bus team. Don't give me that look," he said sharply, noticing Art's and Ben's raised brows. "I'm aware of how that sounds! We're a band of broke dicks in an experimental unit. We're fucking guinea pigs. You know what that makes us? Expendable. We're the fucking expendables! We're also at a level of secrecy so high, I'm dumbfounded anyone in the CIA even knows of our existence. So, what we really need to know is who told them, and why were we requested?" Mac finished his diatribe and once again went mute.

No one spoke. Everyone pondered his words. Even Pavluk, who always had a snarky come-back said nothing.

He downloaded a file to each computer splitting up the task. Quietly, the group began going through the surveillance tapes looking for the two agents and the man wearing glasses.

An hour went by in silence. At ten minutes to midnight, Ben told Art to pause the tape.

"Go back," he said, and then pointing, "there!"

"It's the dude," said Art. "But who's this with him?"

The rest of the team put aside their own computers and leaned in. Art turned the laptop monitor around and hit play. There, the balding man with glasses exited the hotel. The time stamp indicated it was two in the morning. He stopped on the sidewalk and pulled out a cigarette. Another man approached seeming to offer a light. That man was early to mid-thirties, blond, and stern of face. After lighting the cigarette, instead of moving on, the bald man looked around and then tilted his head towards the hotel. He began making his way inside. A few steps behind, the blond man followed. The video time stamp clocked two hours before the blond man exited the hotel, and turning right, walked down the street out of frame.

"Two hours. They met for two hours," said Eastwood. He looked at Pavluk. "Do a crop and send it into command. We need to know who this guy is."

Alex nodded, his good hand making the crop on Art's computer. He sent the crop to his own laptop, and then tapped a few more keys. "I think we found what we needed. We just need to wait for command to get back with us." He stood up, closing his laptop and putting it inside its carry case. "We should get some sleep."

Mac eyed Alex, brow furrowed, and then nodded. Art rubbed his good eye while Ben stretched. Nastjia stood making her way around Alex, keeping her distance. She waited by the door.

"Let us know as soon as you get that message from COM. I feel like we're onto something here," she said.

Eastwood got up, leaning more onto his right leg. It was clear he was in pain, but the big man did not complain. "We're definitely onto something, but like Mac said, the question is what?"

Mac joined Nastjia at the door. Opening it, he let her exit first, then followed her into the hall. Ben and Art went next with Alex pushing between the two of them to leave.

"Damn, Pavluk, we're all tired. No need to be a dick." Art berated the man.

Ben's face twisted in irritation. "Don't waste your breath, Art. He's already down the hall."

Eastwood sighed. "That fucker clearly has some issues. What the hell was that all about? He ran out of here like his ass was on fire."

"I dunno, man. We're all tired. Hopefully we'll get some sleep and some answers." Ben shook his head. "G'night, Harry."

"Yeah. You too. Art, try not to dream about me."

Art chuckled. "Damn right I won't dream about you. I'm looking forward to sweet dreams, not nightmares."

Eastwood chuckled. "Fucker. See you guys in the morning."

The men left. Eastwood closed and locked his door. He got busy running a wire across the bottom of the door frame hooking one end around the hinge and the other end around the leg of the empty twin bed. Then he hung a couple of empty soda cans from the doorknob. If anyone tried getting in, it would make a ruckus and trip the intruder. Safety measures in place, Eastwood removed his pants and unstrapped his prosthetic leg, setting it against the nightstand. He slid a hunting knife purchased at the market under his pillow, and laying down, tried to get some sleep. It didn't come easy. Questions kept popping into his head as he went back over the night's activities. As Morpheus finally began pulling him under, his brain latched onto Pavluk's hasty retreat from his room. It struck him odd, but he couldn't make sense of it, and dreams of Joely beckoned. How could he resist?

❧ ❧

A loud pounding on the door startled Eastwood awake. He jumped up, and then promptly fell sideways catching himself with one hand on the wall. Once stabilized, he grabbed the hunting knife from under his pillow and hopped on his good leg to the door.

"Who is it?" he snarled.

"It's Mac."

Eastwood leaned down and disconnected the trip wire. Unlocking the door, he cracked it open. Seeing Mac on the other side, he let him in. "What is it? What time is it?"

Mac noticed the missing limb. "Sorry about that. It's 0600. We have a problem."

Eastwood hopped back to his bed and grabbed his leg, strapping it on. "What's the problem," he growled.

Mac sat opposite him. "Pavluk is gone."

"What do you mean *gone*?"

Mac sat knees spread, forearms resting on his thighs. Hands clasped, he looked at Eastwood. "About an hour ago he got up saying he needed to piss. Didn't think anything of it and rolled back over. He never came back. When I got up, his stuff was gone. Duffel bag, everything. Gone."

"Did he hear back from command?" Eastwood asked, his brain waking up.

"Dunno." Mac lapsed back into monosyllabic answers.

"Why would he go nomad? You sure he's not in the lobby?" He stood up, looking for his pants.

"Checked already. Not there."

"Shit. Go wake Art and Ben. Have Art contact the major. We need to know if plans have changed. I'll get Nastjia."

Mac left. Eastwood finished getting dressed. He grabbed his carry-kit and keycard and left the room. He made his way down the hall and stopped at Moreno's door. He knocked softly, not wanting to scare the bejesus out of her like Mac did to him.

Despite his soft knock, he heard her curse on the other side of the door. "Who is it?"

A half-smile pulled at his lips as he pictured her on the other side, balancing on one leg, knife in hand. "It's Harry. We have a problem. Pavluk's missing."

"Goddammit," she exclaimed, opening the door. Tired brown eyes met his. "What's that idiot done now?"

"That's what we need to find out. I'll be in the lobby," he said.

Nastjia nodded. "Be there in ten. Gotta piss."

Eastwood left her and joined Art, Ben, and Mac in the lobby. "Any news?"

Art rubbed the side of his face, shaking his head. "I spoke with Major Maxwell. She said she hadn't heard from Pavluk."

"What about results on the facial recognition? Anything?"

Ben and Mac eyed Eastwood, waiting to see his reaction. Art sighed, placing his hands on his hips. "That's just it, Harry. They got the images for the CIA agents and the room occupant, but never got anything on the man he met up with outside the hotel."

"Resend it, then. You still have it on your laptop, don't you?" Eastwood was growing more agitated. The niggling feeling he'd had when falling asleep was now growing into a nagging kick in the ass.

Art shook his head. "Nope. It's been erased. He must've done it when he said he was sending the screenshots to himself. There's no trace of the security footage at all. No sent email in my history."

Nastjia came around the corner, dressed, foot attached, and winding her black hair into a bun at the nape of her neck. She heard the last part. "Don't you still have that other date of footage on your laptop, Harry?"

He nodded. "Should still be there. I never finished looking at it and Pavluk never got his stinkin' fingers on it."

"We need to check it. Now," she said.

"We did get a hit on the balding dude," said Art.

Eastwood turned, heading to his room. The group followed. He glanced over his shoulder. "And?"

"His name is Ari Solomon. He's Mossad," said Art.

They piled into the elevator. Mac snorted.

Nastjia smacked the wall as the elevator doors closed. "What's Israeli intelligence doing involved in all of this?"

"Good question." Eastwood looked at Art. "Did Maxwell have any other info on Solomon?"

The man shrugged. "She said he's been around for at least ten years that our government knows of, but no news on what our agents were doing trailing him. And they wouldn't give up the names of those agents, by the way. Said it was above our paygrade."

"Fuckers," said Mac.

The bell dinged and the doors slid open. As they walked down the hall, Eastwood stopped. Everyone behind him came to an abrupt halt.

Standing outside of his door was the Mossad agent, Ari Solomon.

Eastwood reached for his hunting knife. The act alerted those behind him who fanned out as much as they could in the dark, narrow hallway.

Solomon eyed them; a pale brow raised. "That won't be necessary. We need to talk."

CHAPTER 12

Mac stood by the door. Ben and Art remained standing near him. Eastwood sat opposite Solomon, Nasty to his right on the end of the bed.

Solomon looked at each, assessing the soldiers. "So, it's true," he said. "The Americans really are running a special operations special Olympics."

"Don't be a dick, Ari," said Eastwood. "Yes, we know who you are. What do you want?"

The Mossad agent focused on Eastwood. "You're Harold Tyler, former Green Beret, Staff Sergeant. How's the leg?" His lighthearted tone belied the sarcasm behind his words. It was going to be tit for tat.

Eastwood's eyes narrowed. "How do you know who I am?"

Solomon shrugged. "We have our ways too, Sergeant. Or do you still prefer to be called Eastwood? I'm not sure if you get new codenames in different SOG's."

Eastwood remained quiet, waiting.

"Doesn't matter," said Solomon. "Point is your new unit is compromised. All of you are in danger."

"And why should we believe you? Why would a Mossad agent blow his own cover to warn us?"

Solomon grew serious. "America is still our ally, Sergeant. There was a leak in your State Department recently plugged, or so your command thought. The arrest of Adam Jones was only the tip of the iceberg, I'm afraid."

This was a surprise. Eastwood cursed. "Fucking Jones was the leak?"

"It's been all over your news. Where have you been, Sergeant, under a rock?" Solomon asked.

Eastwood knew exactly where he'd been. Underground, out of touch. Rehab at Camp Lazarus didn't afford any contact with the outside world beyond his weekly phone calls. Apparently, he'd missed a lot. He could just imagine his former commander's reaction to all of this. Outlaw and Jones never got along. The latter was always trying to undermine his captain. There was no single incident that sparked this rivalry. They simply disliked each other from jump. Eastwood suspected it had a lot to do with Jones being such a weak-ass weasel jealous of a real leader who easily commanded respect from his team. Ambition wafted off Jones like a cheap cologne. There wasn't much he wouldn't do to get ahead. It wasn't surprising to find out he'd betrayed his own country.

"Who is he, Harry?" Nasty asked.

"Secretary of State Morgan's aid. Or former aid now, I suppose. A real twat, that one."

"Sounds like you knew him." Solomon chuckled dryly. "But you don't know the extent of his treason. Other players were already in place thanks to Jones. I knew it a month ago. I met a Kremlin operative. He's FSB. Russian military intelligence. He's low-level, though. Still trying to claw his way up the ladder. He came to me with a wild story about wounded warriors patched up and sent back out into the field to run special operations. Universal Soldier types. I didn't believe him, but then he showed me a rendering of a weaponized prosthetic. It was outrageous, of course. Crazy science fiction. I laughed, but he said he got the information from a first-hand source. One of the patched-up soldiers. When I questioned him further, he assured me the source could be trusted. Said it was his own nephew."

The room went quiet.

Anger radiated off Eastwood. He clenched his fist. "And who is this Russian agent?"

Solomon reached into his pocket, extracting a folded piece of paper. He handed it to Eastwood. "Sergei Kolysnik. His official title is emissary for the pro-Russian party here in Ukraine, but his real title is Second Lieutenant Kolysnik, Russian Army. He reports directly back to the FSB. I'm afraid I don't know the name of his nephew yet."

Eastwood threw a look at Mac and the rest of the team. "We do." He turned back to Solomon. "And why are you bothering to share so much information with us? You said we were in danger. From whom?"

Ari Solomon leaned forward. "I knew after your CIA showed up at my hotel something was up. I've been waiting to see who the Americans would send to investigate. Those agents tossed my room, but the only thing they took was that rendering. I had other info tucked away. It was still there where I left it. A thorough search would have led to its discovery, but they'd already found what they were looking for apparently. So, the question is, Sergeant, why did the American military send you and your team of broken toy soldiers in to finish up what the CIA started?"

He let the insult slide, but Eastwood was getting tired of Solomon fast. "I take it you have a theory?"

Solomon stood. "I do. Someone doesn't like you, Sergeant," he said, looking around the room. "Or your team. Someone wants to put an end to your little program."

"Fucking knew it," Mac muttered.

"My guess is that after you all are eliminated, the next target would be your program head. Whoever has invented your fancy props will be next on the list." Solomon rose, squeezing past Nastjia, then stood before Mac at the door. He looked over his shoulder. "As for what I want, Sergeant," he smiled. "I already have it." He looked at Mac who glared at him before stepping aside and letting the man walk out of the room.

"What did he mean by that last crack," asked Ben.

"The plans," Nasty answered. "He already has them. Whether or not he first believed it was true, he knows it now. No way he didn't take pictures of that rendering. No way he didn't show it to his higher-ups. And now he's seen all of us."

Mac cursed and opened the door again. Eastwood stopped him. "It's too late, Mac. Nothing we can do about him now. We need to contact the major ASAP. She needs to know we have a viper in our nest." He looked at the folded paper in his hand. Opening it, he read the information written on it. "Looks like we have a location. Mac, Art, and

Ben, I need you to follow Pavluk. He's surely heading to his uncle's place. Dammit, I knew something wasn't right. My fucking Spidey sense was going off, but I ignored it. He acted all wrong after seeing that CCTV footage. Now I know why. His cover was blown. Fucking little traitorous bastard."

"Don't blame yourself, Harry," said Art. "You'd have to be a damned mind-reader to have known."

"Yeah, man. We know now. We can track him down. He only has about three hours on us. And we know where he's going," said Ben.

Mac looked at them. "Then what are we waiting for?" He turned, heading out of the room.

Art looked at Eastwood. "And what about you and Moreno?"

Eastwood looked at Nasty. "We're flying back to the states. The entire camp is in danger now and we don't know what form that will take. We need to be there. They'll be after Joely—" He stopped himself, and then, "You heard Solomon. They're going to try and take out Ms. Winter. She's a civilian. We protect civilians. Pack up. We move out in thirty."

Joely parked her BMW in the carport of her condo. Living on base during the week was only tolerable because she was able to escape on the weekends here. The three-bedroom unit was in Fairway Hills at The Ridges. With her own private pool and views of the Nevada mountains to the north and golf course nearby, she was able to unwind. Especially after these impromptu trips to D.C. She hated being at the beck and call of the State Department, but with the contract between her business, WinRunner, and the Department of Defense, it couldn't be helped. It was late on a Friday. She locked the car and pulled her rolling Louis Vuitton suitcase behind her.

She had the whole weekend before she needed to make the two and a half-hour drive back up US95 to Groom Lake, known to alien-loving science fiction fans as Area 51. It'd been a week since Harry deployed. There'd been no updates on his mission, not that she expected one. Major Sydelle Maxwell didn't answer to her and she'd been afraid to ask. It wouldn't be good for anyone to suspect her relationship with Harry. And even if Syd did suspect, she didn't need to provide confirmation. Still, she missed him, and she was worried sick.

Cool air greeted her inside the twenty-four-thousand square foot condominium. The tiled floor and soothing shades of gray and cream accented by natural wood beams and a slate fireplace relaxed her bringing a little peace to her over-worked soul. The views of the mountains from both her living room and master suite made the $1.4 million property worth the purchase.

As she shed her heels by the kitchen island, the thought occurred that she'd like to bring Harry here. Once he graduated rehab fully, he'd be eligible for living off-base. Maybe while he looked for a place of his own, he could stay in one of the two spare bedrooms. But she knew that wouldn't last. He might unpack in a spare room, but he'd be warming her bed and satisfying all her lady parts in the master suite. A slow smile spread across her red lips. Their night together a week ago reminded her just what an amazing lover he was. She knew it in London, but their wild weekend had been cut short when her best friend Emma got kidnapped. She didn't bother to seek him out after Nate rescued Emma, and because of her new obligations with the DOD, she'd missed Emma's wedding. Becky stood up with her and Dina attended. Both poo-pooed her, and rightly so, but she tried making up for it by sending Emma and Nate on an all-expenses paid honeymoon to Playa Del Carmen. Between the Sangria, the tacos, and the blinding-white sands of the resort's pristine beach, she was forgiven. But she'd missed out on seeing Harry again.

It was a twist of fate that brought them together, and one she'd gladly give up if it meant Harry could have his leg back. But she couldn't control fate, and it apparently was not finished with her yet. Making love with him last week began purely as a means to bolster his confidence before the mission—or so she told herself. It ended in orgasmic ecstasy and heart-melting intimacy. Harry could be very sweet and incredibly gentle for such a big, strong man. She liked that he didn't take her shit. And she'd tried. For months, Joely made every effort to maintain a professional distance. She'd ignored his heated stares. Left every room when he came in. Sat on the opposite side of the conference room during briefings and medical updates. None of it stopped her body from getting hot and bothered, and he'd noticed, damn him! When his sexy green eyes raked over her curves, her nipples hardened instantly. When he smiled, she grew moist. Twice she'd had to remove herself to her own quarters and relieve the sexual tension manually. Her vibrator wasn't nearly as satisfying as Harry.

Even thinking of him now while pouring a glass of Merlot she felt the familiar tingles.

Joely watched the stars twinkling in the Nevada sky through her picture window, and then, downing the last of her glass of wine, headed to her room. It had been a long day, and she was ready for a shower and her bed.

She turned off the hall light and walked to her room. She went straight to the ensuite, turning on the shower. As steam filled the large bathroom, she re-entered her bedroom in search of her robe. Hands grabbed her from behind, one clamping over her mouth. She kicked and tried to scream, but a chemical smell filled her nostrils and her vision dimmed, going black.

CHAPTER 13

I t took twenty-three hours to get back into the U.S. In that time, Eastwood and Nastjia researched everything they could find on Sergei Kolysnik. According to the PATCH database, which uplinked to the Spec Ops data at Fort Bragg, the State Department had received him twice diplomatically. Kolysnik had traveled to the U.S. with the Russian Ambassador, Dmitri Antonov both times in the past year. There were two Ukrainian articles mentioning him at pro-Russian Party fundraising events, but beyond that, nothing. It seemed he was a new player recently ascending to the field. It made sense seeing as how the man appeared to be no more than thirty-to-thirty-two years of age. It was likely he'd been making his bones in the Russian military before now. Even so, to rise to enough prominence to travel with the Russian ambassador meant he'd done something extraordinary to gain the Kremlin's attention.

What Eastwood and Moreno both wanted to know was why did he sell the weaponized warrior plans to a Mossad agent? Why not give them to his own government?

Eastwood tabled those questions. They rented a car at the airport terminal. Someone from the base could return it the next day. For now, he needed to get back to Joely. His gut told him something was wrong. Solomon's casual mention of the imminent danger to the person responsible for inventing their unique prosthetics didn't set well with him. As an Israeli agent, he surely had access to information that would lead an intelligence officer to WinRunner, and its founder, Joely Winter. And if Mossad had that info, so did the Russians.

The drive up to Area 51 was two-and-a-half hours. Not knowing whether she was safe for that much longer ate at him.

He turned to Moreno who was loading her duffel bag into the backseat of the Chevy Impala. "Call the Major. Tell her we're on our way." For the last ten hours, they'd been out of contact with command.

He slid into the driver's seat, carefully pulling in his prosthetic leg. The stump throbbed from the long hours traveling, but it was getting more tolerable. Beside Eastwood, Nastjia put on her seatbelt and then pulled out her burner phone. When she turned it on, it pinged, indicating missed calls.

"Looks like she's been trying to call us." She hit the button for voicemail and listened. Her expression changed from calm to alarmed.

"What is it?" he asked.

Nastjia shook her head. "The major wants us to call her ASAP. Says she can't find Joely."

Eastwood slammed on the brake. "What? Give me that," he said, snatching the phone from her hand. He hit redial.

The major answered on the first ring. "Dammit, Moreno, what took you so long?"

"It's Tyler. And we just got off the plane and into a rental car, ma'am. What's going on?"

Major Maxwell got right to the point. "We followed up on the information you sent over regarding Pavluk. His uncle was never listed in his file. Only his immediate family. Mother and Father. Alex naturalized to citizenship through his service, but his parents never completed their own journey to becoming citizens. We didn't know about his mother's family connections because she gave a fake maiden name on her application when they defected here. It took quite a bit of research these last eighteen hours just to put two and two together. If the U.S. had facial recognition software in the early eighties, we would've caught it then. As it was, Eigenface recognition didn't come into play until well after 1988. Point is, no one knew he was related to the Kolysniks. His grandfather was a major in the Russian army. A decorated war veteran who went on to advise some of the top politicians in the Kremlin before his death in the early nineties. He was part of the anti-Gorbachev movement. Thing is, when his beloved daughter defected, he cut her off. That included Alex. It wasn't until after both the old man and Pavluk's father died that he reconnected with them. We found phone records and letters. Based on that, we believe he's used some of his time away on assignment to visit the uncle. I knew there'd been some questionable time entries in his reports, but he's always completed his missions with success."

Eastwood listened, growing more frustrated by the minute. "Major, that's all very interesting, but what about Joely Winter?"

"We can't locate her. She arrived back last night from D.C. I tried calling. We needed her input on Alex's mental state and any red flags she could think of, but she never answered. I'm here at her place now. Her bags are here.

She's not. I need you to get over here. I've been given to understand you two knew each other from before?"

Eastwood squirmed in his seat. "Back in London. My former commander's wife, before she was his wife, was kidnapped by Black Jihad. Joely and Emma are friends," he said, sticking to the simplest explanation.

"Good. I need you to reach out to her friends. See if she's contacted any of them. We'll be checking the community's security cameras too for clues. I'm sending the address now. Hurry," she said, and then hung up.

"Well?" Nastjia asked, impatiently.

He handed her the cell phone. "Enter that address into the GPS. We're meeting Maxwell at Joely's."

Nastjia typed in the address and hit start. "She's really missing then?"

"Looks that way." Eastwood chewed his lip. "Goddammit. If Pavluk harms her, I'm going to kill him!" He slammed his fist on the steering wheel.

"We don't know if he has her, Harry. Take a chill pill. When you lose control of your temper, you lose control of the situation. You know this."

He maneuvered the Impala into traffic, heading north. "Who else would it be, Moreno?"

She thought about it. "Alex is a lot of things. A real asshole for one. A needy little bastard too. He doesn't handle rejection well, but Ms. Winter has always treated him kindly and he likes her. I don't think he'd do her any harm."

"I'm not so sure about that," said Eastwood. "But if not Pavluk, then who?"

She looked at him. "Solomon said someone else wanted us out of the picture, wanted the inventor gone. His uncle took those renderings to Mossad instead of his own people. Do you think it's FSB? Maybe the Russians?"

"Doesn't make sense. If they were pissed at Kolysnik for selling to the Israelis then they'd simply take him out, not us. Not Joely."

"We're missing something here, Harry. I know it."

"Me, too. But I've a shitty feeling we're going to find out, and not like it at all." He jumped lanes and sped past a slow-moving truck. As he drove, Eastwood's thoughts turned to Joely. Wherever she was, he hoped like hell she was still alive. *Hold on, baby. I'm coming!*

❦

Cool air blew in Joely's face. Her neck hurt and her mouth was as dry as the desert. She licked her lips and tried opening her eyes. Light poured in blinding her temporarily.

She blinked and focused. All she saw was a low ceiling. A vent overhead was pumping cool air into the room. She straightened her neck. Coming to, she realized she was tied to a chair, arms behind her back. Her head had lolled back stretching her neck and putting a kink in the muscles. Her knees screamed too, bent back with her ankles tied to the chair legs. All she wanted to do was stretched her limbs and drink some water, but neither was going to happen. She'd been taken and she had no idea by who or why.

She looked around the room. It appeared to be a hotel room, and not a cheap one if the art hanging before her was any indicator. Maybe a suite. She faced the wall so could not see either the door or the window. Joely looked left and right, desperately trying to orient herself and gather some visual clues. There was a queen-sized bed covered in a blue damask duvet. A phone sat on the nightstand. Hope filled her. If she could just get to it.

She flexed her fingers, testing the wrist restraints. She could move her hands, but not much. Perhaps enough to dial 9-1-1 if she could just get herself over to the nightstand. Pins and needles immediately stabbed her fingers, hands, and arms. The pain was excruciating. She took a deep breath until it subsided. Then, with as much effort as she could muster, she attempted to scoot the chair. On the thick carpet, it moved only an inch. The hard wood and upholstery made the chair heavy. She redoubled her effort and tried again. This time she moved a couple of inches in the right direction.

Another hop woke up her numb feet. More pins and needles. She ignored them and moved again. She was almost to the end of the bed when the door opened.

Two large men moved to either side of the chair. One pointed a gun in her face while the other grabbed the arm of the chair and pulled her back to the middle of the room.

Tears welled in Joely's blue eyes, but she blinked them away. She would not give them the satisfaction of seeing her cry.

"I see you are awake, Ms. Winter." A voice came from behind, the accent subtle but recognizable.

She craned her neck trying to see the owner. A man stepped into her field of vision to stand before her. He was early to mid-thirties, blond, and well-dressed. His slate-colored suit was accented by a silver and blue tie. The tie clasp pinning it to his crisp white shirt was the white, blue, and red of the Russian Federation flag.

Joely swallowed. She'd been taken by Russians. Why?

"And who the hell are you?"

His thin lips spread into a smile, but it didn't reach his cold eyes. "A feisty one, as they say." He unbuttoned his suit jacket and slid his hands into his pants pockets. "I am Sergei Kolysnik. You would, no doubt, never have heard of me, but you know my nephew well. Alexei has spoken of you."

Her mind spun. Alexei. That's Alex. The only Alex she knew was... "Pavluk? Your nephew is Alex Pavluk?"

"Da," he said.

"I don't understand. What the hell is going on? Why have you kidnapped me? Where's Alex?"

He held up a hand. "Calm yourself. We have business, you and I. That business will answer all of your questions, Joely Winter." He snapped his fingers and the big mercenary on her right left the room. He returned with a bottle of water which he held to her mouth.

Joely gulped down the cool liquid.

"I am not without care for your current state. Ether leaves a nasty after-taste and I need you to be able to speak, to focus." Sergei moved forward, squatting down before her. "You are, unfortunately, finding yourself in the middle of the business of men, of governments. While I admire your work, it is causing unrest in the Kremlin's investment."

"What are you talking about?"

Kolysnik continued. "The weaponized prosthetics you have invented are impressive but putting these Humpty Dumpty soldiers back together and sending them out into the field is bad for Nightwing Enterprises."

"Never heard of it."

"Nightwing, Ms. Winter, is the financial arm of Blackwater."

Joely's eyes widened. "The mercenary group?" She glanced at the two big men.

"The one and the same," he answered. "Countries like mine, Israel, Turkey, Pakistan, Saudi Arabia, Ukraine, and even your allies, France, Britain, as well as the United States all hire mercenaries. My country started Nightwing to have a controlling interest in the business of mercenaries. It's quite lucrative. The return on such an investment goes beyond rubles as you can imagine. Leverage is often the greater value. Then, when Alexei reconnected with his family it brought new opportunity. Not at first. Not until he was injured. When he came around six months ago, we shared drink and he showed me his shiny new arm and leg. Imagine my surprise to discover its hidden weapons capability. Even more surprising, the drink loosened his tongue further and he spilled a few secrets regarding your PATCH-COM program. As a loyal soldier of Mother Russia and admittedly, an ambitious man, I took this information to my higher ups. Unfortunately for you, they were not interested in broken soldiers. My government does not want to see anything happen to its investment. There will be no competition. But there was still fortune to be made for me in selling useless plans to Israel."

One word stood out. "You said useless plans. What do you mean by that?"

He smirked. "Well, not entirely useless, which brings me to the point of our business. I want all your plans. All the schematics. Once you give me what I ask for, our business will be concluded."

Something in the way he framed his words sent chills down her spine. Joely had a bad feeling that by concluded, he meant she would be concluded. As in dead.

"I don't have my plans on me, Sergei."

He stood. "No, I did not think that you would, but you invented them." He nodded to the mercenary who'd brought her water. He turned her chair around. A small table with blank paper and some pens sat before her.

"You want me to draw for you?" Her eyebrows arched in surprise.

"So simple, don't you agree? Of course, we could conclude our business now, without the drawings." The man behind her tapped the back of her head with the barrel of the gun.

Fear shot through her. Her mind raced along with her heart. Somehow, she needed to delay, to find a way to get to that phone. She closed her eyes and prayed. "Okay. You win. I'll draw my prosthetics for you."

"Good. You are a smart woman. I expect them all, with great details on the weapons systems."

She tugged at her restraints. "I need my hands."

"Of course," he nodded to the gunman who pulled out a large, sharp knife.

Joely sucked in a breath as he sliced through the zip-ties. The pins and needles were immediate. She gripped her hands, wringing and shaking them. Tears stung her eyes, but she pushed back the pain. "Please, would you release my feet as well? I don't think I can concentrate on drawing through the pain."

Sergei eyed her. Joely blew out a frustrated breath.

"For God's sakes, what can I possibly do? You have two big thugs here with a gun on me. I don't even know where the hell I am!"

Kolysnik gave in. Once her feet were unbound, he moved to the door, glancing back at her. "Don't try anything. I'll be back in one hour. I expect you to be finished." He looked at the gunman. "Anders can handle a single woman. I need you with me." The gunman followed Sergei out of the room.

Joely was left with the one called Anders. She pulled a piece of paper in front of her. It was hotel stationary. The logo read High Desert Villas. She knew this place, had passed it a couple of times. They were high end villas often used by celebrities for their secure location. If she could get to the phone, she'd be able to call the base, get help. She thought of Harry. More than anything she wanted him to bust through the door and save the day like his commander did back in London for her friend Emma. But Harry was on the other side of the world. Too far away to help, and no one knew she was missing. A tear escaped sliding down her cheek. She would have to save herself, and she needed to do it quickly. She had less than an hour to live.

CHAPTER 14

The footage rolled showing black and white images of a car pulling into Joely's driveway. She got out and then pulled a large suitcase out of the trunk. Vuitton. Of course. Joely liked her labels. Just a woman arriving home from a trip. Nothing abnormal about it except for the earlier footage. Eastwood snapped a rubber band wrapped around his wrist repeatedly. Beside him, Major Maxwell, Moreno, and Jackson all stared at the tiny screen inside the condominium complex's guard house. The coroner left having been called in to take away the body—the guard who'd been on duty the night before. Local police grumbled when the FBI arrived claiming jurisdiction over the murder of the security guard and now, the abduction of Joely Winter.

Before she'd come home, another car approached the gate. Not having a way in otherwise, it had to stop at the gatehouse. When the guard came out to the driver's side, an explosion of light in the black and white video recorded the moment the gun went off point blank in the man's face. His name was Edward Turner. He was a retired patrol officer, and this was his part-time job to make ends meet on social security. The driver jumped out and hauled the remains of Mr. Turner inside the guard house. He opened the gate and returned to the dark SUV, driving into the small community of private villas. This same vehicle drove out of the opposite gate less than twenty minutes after Joely walked into her home.

"Go back to the first segment when they come in," said Jackson.

FBI agent Jake Matthews stood behind them. Next to him was Special Agent Reid Warren. The two men looked every inch a G-man from their black-rimmed glasses to their nearly matching dark suits.

Moreno rewound back to the scene of the murder. Right before the gun went off, Jackson said, "There. Freeze it!"

Nastjia hit pause.

"What are we looking at?" asked the Major.

Eastwood leaned forward, pointing. "That," he said. His eyes took in the driver's forearm. A black snake tattoo wound around the limb. He'd seen it before. He spat out a curse. "The merc on my transport!"

"What?" Major Maxwell looked at him. "What are you saying, Sergeant?"

Surprise and anger mixed into a terrifying expression on Eastwood's face. "The goddamned mercenary. He was on my flight in. He was here when me and Art and Matt were brought in. I knew I knew that tattoo. There were two of them. I'd bet good money the other was in the SUV with him."

Agent Matthews shared a look with Special Agent Warren. "Why would the military hire mercenaries for transport? Major?"

Sydelle Maxwell shook her head. "We don't. As least, I've never been privy to it. This doesn't make sense. Sergeant Tyler, are you absolutely certain?"

Eastwood nodded. "With all due respect, Major, there's nothing wrong with my brain. I know what I saw. That's a unique tattoo."

"And why did you call him a mercenary," she asked. "How do you know this?"

"I know the type. Remember, I came from the field. I've worked around them. I know a mercenary when I see one. Ex-military men who can't cut in under a regulated command. There's something about them that's more broken than any of us," he said, looking at Moreno and Jackson. "They get a taste for killing and they want more. Then they find out they can make money being murderers for hire. They have no honor. It struck me as odd when I arrived, but until now, honestly, I'd forgotten about them. But this isn't a coincidence," he said, looking at the screen.

Special Agent Warren nodded in agreement. "You're right about that. Can you zoom in on the license plate?" he asked Moreno.

She punched a few keys and the license plate filled the small screen.

"Diplomatic plates," said Warren. He glanced at his partner. "Russian."

"What the fuck?" Eastwood's head spun. Why would mercenaries hired by Russians go after Joely? He remembered Ari Solomon's words. Someone didn't like their group. Someone wanted to put an end to PATCH-COM. That someone knew an awful lot about them. Knew about their top-secret group, where they were located. That list was small. Someone on that list was losing something of value by their very existence, and in Eastwood's experience, that something of value was always money. Money was the biggest motive for murder there was outside of lust and revenge. And somewhere in that mix was Alex Pavluk.

Agents Matthews and Warren took a picture of the screen and then, pulled the plug from the wall. The screen went black.

"We'll take it from here, Major Maxwell, and we'll let you know when we find something." Special Agent Warren threw a look at Matthews who immediately pulled the disk from the slot, pocketing it.

"Hold on, Agent Warren," the Major began. "We're just as invested into investigating this. Joely Winter is part of our team."

"Yeah, you can't cut us out," said Eastwood.

"We can and we have," said Matthews. "This is a federal investigation now. It did not happen on military property. This is civilian ground and abductions are the jurisdiction of the bureau. You're ordered to stand down. We have the helm on this one."

Matthews and Warren left, the discussion at an end.

"There's no fucking way we're not going after her, Major. Please tell me you're not going to let them order you around?"

Syd's eyes narrowed. She remained quiet, thinking. Finally, "I think I made myself clear, Sergeant. Joely Winter is part of our team. We do not leave a teammate behind."

She looked at Jackson. "I know we didn't give you that eye for nothing, Hicks. Tell me you remember the license plate on that security footage."

Jackson smiled, slow and sweet as you please. "And the make and model of the SUV, too."

The major nodded. "Write it down. I'll call it into the base. We can have Las Vegas traffic cameras hacked in under ten minutes. We'll find where they went."

Eastwood regarded his commander. "Damn, Major, you are one badass—"

"Shut yo mouth!" she said, then smirked, looking at her team. "We'll find her."

❧❦

Joely felt a trickle of sweat slide down her spine. She'd made three renderings, but there were at least fifteen different designs. She'd left out important pieces of the puzzle in each one. There was no way she'd give her real plans to the Russians. What did it matter if she was going to die anyhow? But she didn't want to die. Didn't plan on it.

The only problem with that plan was figuring how to save herself.

The guard called Anders sat on the bed with his feet propped up, leaning on the headboard. The phone was on the nightstand next to him. He stared at the wall, but now and again his eyes closed, and his head lolled before he jerked awake again.

She bent over the drawing pretending to concentrate but cast her eyes about the room looking for a weapon or a distraction. Anything. All she saw were a few decorations. A vase with fake flowers. A lamp on a small side table. These things would work well enough to slam onto a person's head, but she'd have to get to them first. The odds of outrunning an armed mercenary seemed practically nil. Overpowering him would never happen. Despair hit and it hit hard. Time was running out. She closed her eyes and thought of Harry. There were so many things she wished she'd said. Like how proud she was of him for overcoming the loss of his leg with such grace and dignity. A lot of soldiers can't handle the loss. They struggle, but Harry managed. And he made her laugh. Despite every effort to keep her distance, he still managed to reel her in. He was patient. Kind. Smart. And sexy as hell. And she wouldn't get the chance to tell him how she felt.

A soft snore sounded behind her.

Joely glanced over at the guard. He'd fallen asleep. This was her chance. She had to make it count.

Sliding her chair back, she stood. It took a moment to steady her limbs. She was still wearing her travel clothes. Navy slacks, a short-sleeved sweater in cream, but no shoes. Not exactly what a gal hoped to be wearing during a fight for her life. Thankfully, the carpet muted her footsteps. She decided against trying to cosh the guard's head. Instead, she would make a run for it. There'd been no sound from the next room since Sergei Kolysnik left. She surmised the room she was in was part of a suite. If she could get out of this bedroom without waking the guard, she would run like hell.

Another snore made her pause. She dared a look back. The man was listing over to one side in a slow-motion slide. Any moment now he would hit the pillow and wake. She told her feet to move. Carefully, she turned the door handle and pulled it open. Slipping through, she closed it behind her. She was in a living room. She looked for the main door and then took off running. A loud curse emitted from the bedroom followed by heavy footsteps. Fear shot through her. Adrenaline fueled her mad dash to the door. As she reached forward, she heard the bedroom door open behind her.

She grabbed the doorknob, throwing the door wide and stopped dead in her tracks. The barrel of a Sig Sauer 9mm pointed straight at her face. She opened her mouth to scream. A hand roughly pushed her down. Shots fired, the sound deafening. The smell of gunpowder scented the air. A loud thud from behind made her jump and the silence that followed was interrupted by the ringing in her ears.

She lay against the wall, huddled in on herself, shaking violently. Terror gripped her and she was afraid to look up. A hand touched her shoulder and she jerked.

"Ms. Winter."

She knew the voice.

"Ms. Winter, we have to go."

Slowly, Joely turned looking up. "Please don't hurt me."

"I'm not here to hurt you, but we need to go. Now."

Joely cautiously took Alex Pavluk's hand. His face was hard, his expression neutral.

She rose on unsteady legs.

"Come on. We don't have much time. He'll be back any minute."

She followed him out to the driveway. "Alex, we need to call for help."

He reached into his pocket and pulled out a burner, tossing it to her. "Call whoever you wish but do it while moving."

He walked fast down the driveway sighting left and right. Joely attempted to keep up while trying to remember a phone number Any number! All her important numbers were in her cell phone. *Damned technology. Before cell phones, I could remember a freaking number because I had to actually dial it*, she thought.

The only number that came to mind was the main phone line into the base. That would work. They could patch her through. She punched in the number.

"Stop!" Alex froze.

Joely bounced off his back. "What?"

Headlights came at them. The engine accelerated.

"Run!" Alex grabbed Joely's hand and took off.

She stumbled trying to keep up, rocks digging into her bare feet. The burner phone flew from her grasp landing somewhere on the ground behind them.

Alex cut around the side of the villa heading for the open desert beyond the reach of the property's lights. "We can lose them in the dark. Don't look back. Just run," he said.

Her lungs burned but she ran, ignoring her own pain. The car stopped. She heard doors slam and boots running.

"Get them!"

It was Kolysnik.

Shots fired. Alex reached out and grabbed the back of Joely's neck. "Get low!"

They ran in the dark, Alex leading the way. He pulled her behind two large boulders. Bullets bounced off the rocks. Alex returned fire.

"Alexei!" Kolysnik shouted.

Silence filled the void. Sergei and the mercenary stopped shooting.

"What!" Alex leaned against the boulder, his eyes searching the darkness.

"We are family, Alexei. The woman is not worth this. Come. Join me."

Joely reached out, touching Alex's shoulder. "He's lying. He's just trying to lure you out and then he'll kill you. Kill us."

Pavluk looked at her. His eyes gentled. "I know, Ms. Winter. I'm trained to know these tricks, remember?"

"Alex, why are you here?" She'd been wondering this since the moment she'd thrown open the door of the villa to flee.

"That's my uncle Sergei, Ms. Winter. My mother's youngest brother. Before my parents defected, he and I grew up together as close as brothers. But after my mother left her family behind, they disowned her. It wasn't until after my father died that I reached out to them. I was already an adult then. They welcomed me back, but still never forgave my mother until the day she died. I'm ashamed to admit that I visited them while on assignment a few times. I shouldn't have, but I didn't want to miss the opportunity when I was so close to my grandmother's home. It was great at first, but after seeing the video tape in Kiev of him meeting with the Mossad agent, Solomon, I knew it was my own foolishness that led to the leak. I knew then Sergei lied to me about being an accountant. He took advantage of my desire to be with family again. This is my fault. So, I went after him. I have to clean up my own mess. You and my brothers and sisters at Camp Lazarus are my family. I just realized it too late. Can you forgive me?"

Tears welled in Joely's eyes. "Alex, of course I forgive you. You saved my life."

He smiled, but it didn't reach his eyes. "Not yet."

The sound of car doors slamming in the distance was drowned out by gunfire. This time, the bullets were aimed back at the villa.

"Looks like the cavalry has arrived," said Alex. He positioned himself at the edge of the boulder. He glanced at Joely. "Tell the major and the men I'm sorry. And tell Nastjia..." He fell silent.

"What? Tell her what, Alex? What are you going to do?" Alarm bells went off in her head.

"There's no excuse, but please, tell her I was drunk. Should've never tried to kiss her. I'm sorry." He ran out into the dark, gun blazing.

Sergei Kolysnik turned, aimed, and fired. Alex went down.

"Alex!" she screamed.

Kolysnik ran at her. From behind, a large man barreled after him. There was a familiarity in his gait. Shots fired striking Kolysnik in the back. He fell face-first into the Nevada dust.

Joely could barely see him in the moonlight but he wasn't moving.

"Joely?"

That voice! "Harry!" She scrambled onto her feet and ran to him. "Harry?"

"Joely! Baby, I'm here!"

Strong arms wrapped around her waist lifting her off her feet. She buried her face in his neck and held on for dear life. The tears she'd held back spilled down her cheeks.

"Hey, hey, hey," he said, rubbing her back. He set her down on her own two feet. With gentle hands, he cradled her face. "It's okay. You're okay. I'm here, baby. I'm here."

"Oh my God, Harry," she wailed, gripping his shoulders. "How?"

"It's a long story. Are you okay?" He looked her over from head to toe.

She nodded, sniffing loudly. "Yes, I'm not harmed." She touched his bearded cheek. "You came for me."

He leaned his forehead to hers. "Of course. I'll always come for you, baby."

"Oh, Harry," she kissed his lips, her emotions raw.

Surprised, he kissed her back taking advantage of the darkness. It was sweet yet savage. Passionate, but healing. And full of words unsaid. Finally, he pulled back.

"We should—"

"Yes, we should," she agreed, catching her breath. "Harry, we need to get to Alex. He saved my life."

"What?"

"He saved me from his uncle," she said, tugging his hand. "He was trying to clean up his mess, he said. Oh, Harry, he wasn't a traitor. He was just desperate for family." She pulled Eastwood toward Pavluk who lay motionless on the ground.

Eastwood kneeled and checked for a pulse.

"Is he alive?"

He looked at Joely, shaking his head. "He's gone."

Fresh tears blurred her vision and grief shook her. "All he wanted was to belong, to have family. He said he was sorry. Kolysnik told me Alex was drunk. That dirty bastard took advantage of his own nephew, his own family, for profit."

"Sometimes your greatest enemy is the one you never suspect." Eastwood placed a hand on Alex's head and said a quick prayer. He didn't like Pavluk, but he could admit he never tried, never understood the man. Still, he was forever grateful that he saved Joely. To that end, Alex was a hero.

Standing, Eastwood took Joely's hand and led her back to the edge of the villa grounds. The FBI showed up taking over the scene. An ambulance arrived and took Kolysnik away, handcuffed to the gurney.

"I can't believe he's still alive," said Joely.

Major Maxwell sighed. "If he lives, he won't even face consequences."

"Why not," she asked.

Eastwood growled, "Fucking diplomatic immunity. The Kremlin will demand him back."

Nastjia and Jackson joined them. Joely hugged them both and whispered in Nastjia's ear. The woman straightened her spine, sniffed, and walked away.

"What's wrong with Moreno," Jackson asked.

"Dunno," said Eastwood. "Joely?" he raised a questioning eyebrow.

"It's private." She felt suddenly weary. "Harry, I just want to go home."

He looked at his commander. Major Maxwell nodded, a small smile on her lips. "You're dismissed, Sergeant. But I expect you both back at base at 0700 for debriefing."

Jackson grinned and, whistling, fell in with Maxwell who made her way back to the car.

Eastwood watched them go. "Baby, I think they know."

She leaned against his side. "Yeah. Pretty sure they do. Now what are we going to do about it?"

He looked down into her blue eyes. "Well, I have a few ideas."

"I bet you do, but not tonight."

"No, not tonight," he sighed, exhausted. "Tonight, I'd like to just hold you in my arms if that's okay."

"There's nowhere else I'd rather be, Harry."

CHAPTER 15

A month passed since her insane abduction. Joely glowed with happiness. Following the command's debriefing of the Pavluk/Kolysnik affair, as it was named, Harry received his patch. The ceremony made his graduation official. He was now a member of an elite unit of specialized men and women, again. The blue and white patch was pinned to the sleeve of his uniform. The flaming skull was surrounded by the words *PATCH-COM, Never Say Die, Hoorah and Rise!*

With graduation came the privilege of living off base. Joely invited Harry to stay at her place until he could find one of his own. A few days grew into a week, and a week grew into a month of making love, cooking dinners, laughing. She didn't think she could possibly be happier.

She danced around the kitchen while making dinner. Harry was at a meeting that didn't involve her end of things. That suited her just fine. It gave her time to plan out a meal of Italian stuffed shells, salad, and Sangria. It was their anniversary. Two months since their wild night reconnecting like wild animals. While the shells baked, she changed into a slinky bronze sheath and leopard Louboutin stilettos. She felt sexy and couldn't wait for her man to get home.

My man, she thought, grinning.

She checked herself in the mirror, fluffing her long, blonde hair, and then returned to the kitchen. On the way, she straightened the living room, taking time to place Harry's reading glasses on top a copy of a Lonesome Dove novel. She discovered he loved old westerns and enjoyed reading. Remembering how he looked as he quietly thumbed through the well-worn book made her smile. Looking at him, no one would think the muscled soldier used to handling every kind of weapon would be a reader, but Harry was definitely a bookworm. He also liked to bake. Mostly cookies, which he ate before they had time to cool, but that was another adorable facet to this man. His mom, he said, was quite the baker of goodies. He missed her. That was obvious. Now that he was above ground again, he could call her on his own cell phone. Seeing him interact with

Meredith Tyler warmed her heart. *You could always tell a good man by how he treats his mom*, she thought, and Harry loved his mom.

Joely was surprised, though, when he told Meredith about her.

"I met someone special, mom. You'll like her. Her name's Joely Winter," he said, winking. *"She's a real pip just like someone else I know."*

That was two days ago. Since then, Harry had been acting differently. She couldn't put her finger on it, but he was keeping something from her. She planned on getting it out of him tonight. She didn't like secrets. He was either going to tell her voluntarily, or, she'd seduce it out of him.

The timer dinged. The shells were ready. She glanced at her watch. Harry was late.

⁘⁘⁘⁘⁘⁘

Eastwood stood in the conference room; shock written all over his face. Next to him, Moreno, Jackson, Matt, Ben, Art, and Mac all stood at attention.

"Atten-SHUN," Major Maxwell announced.

General P.K. Davidson strode into the room, a bear of a man with a disposition to match. He knew the general well. He oversaw Eastwood's old special operations group. His former commander, Captain Nathan James Oliver, known in the field as Outlaw, answered directly to him.

General Davidson positioned himself at the head of the conference table looking around the room. "I'll make this short," he said. "Much has happened since the Kolysnik affair. Investigations revealed a traitor in our midst. That traitor has been dealt with according to military code. Colonel Ambrose Carnahan will be court martialed at the first of the year. In the meantime, he'll remain housed in federal penitentiary."

Moreno gasped.

"Yes, Petty Officer Moreno. That was my reaction too. Ambrose came up under my command. To find out he's betrayed his own for money is sickening. I won't go into details but suffice to say that the mercenaries you all helped take down were part of the colonel's retirement plan. He sold us out to the goddamned Kremlin. Fucking Russians!" General Davidson clenched his fists.

Eastwood looked at Ben and Art. Matt and Jackson shook their heads in disbelief.

Mac snorted under his breath, "Knew it."

"Now," the general continued. "There's going to be a few changes at PATCH-COM."

"What changes, sir?" Eastwood asked.

The general glanced his way, squinting. "Eastwood, good to see you, son. How's the leg?"

Eastwood leaned down and knocked it. "Solid, sir."

"Good. Glad to hear it. Goddamned shame what happened to you, but you've bounced back. I knew you would. Knew this would be good for you."

This was news to Eastwood. He'd long wondered how he ended up at Camp Lazarus. Now he knew.

"As I was saying, some changes are coming up. Israel wants in."

Eastwood blinked.

"I guess you made quite the impression on the Mossad agent, Sergeant." The General's words were complimentary, but his tone and expression weren't. "I though you boys were supposed to be invisible out in the field. How the hell you caught the eye of Mossad, I'd like to know. But we'll save that for another day. Our program here has proven successful. The fact that some of our allies now want a slice of the pie shouldn't take away from what you've accomplished. Be proud, and then prepare. A new group of potentials will be arriving after the holidays. We've negotiated one from each of our major allies. Canada, Israel, Great Britain, and France. This is a probationary exchange. One fuck-up from any of them and they're out. I still expect all of you to be at your best and help where you can. At the end of the day, they're all soldiers, all wounded warriors, and that alone demands our respect. Is everyone clear?"

Major Maxwell answered, "Sir, yes sir."

"Oh, and one last thing. We've made an enemy. With your continued success comes greater danger now from the countries not invited to participate in this venture of ours. Russia won't forgive us for building this elite special force. It cuts into their bottom line in the mercenary business. While I do enjoy pissing off the Kremlin every day of the week, I don't like knowing that with this new exposure, your jobs are more dangerous than usual. You all need to be extra vigilant when next you're sent out on assignment, and every mission thereafter. Understood?"

"Sir, yes sir," they answered.

The general nodded and turned. The group raised their hands, holding the salute. Davidson gave a perfunctory return salute as he walked around the table. He stopped in front of Eastwood.

"The men miss you, son. You have my permission to give Nate a call. Check in. Just stick to protocol if he asks too many questions. He'll understand. He's got a lot to tell you. Probably bore you to death with baby stories." He patted

Eastwood's shoulder. "Really glad you're doing well. It's good to have you back under my command."

The general left. Eastwood pondered his words. Emma had the baby. Outlaw was a dad, and he had more to tell him. His heart hurt thinking about all he'd missed with Doc, Skyscraper, Hollywood, Ghost, and Outlaw. He hoped to see them again someday, but at least for now, he could call and catch up. Glancing at his watch he realized it was after four. He still had a two-and-a-half-hour drive home. Joely said dinner would be ready at six. He was going to be late. Damn. She was going to be pissed. And he still had one stop to make.

CHAPTER 16

The tap-tapping of a leopard Louboutin greeted him as he walked through the door. It wasn't a happy tap. He was over an hour late. His sweaty palms belied the cheery expression he immediately pasted on his face.

"Hey, baby. Dinner ready?"

A spoon flew at major league speed straight at his head. He ducked and it bounced off the door.

"Don't you *Hey Baby* me, Harold Tyler! What the hell? Can't pick up a phone?" Joely stood, hands on hips, and furious as a wet cat.

She never looked more beautiful. He took in the bronze-colored dress, the material as thin as lingerie and clinging to every curve. Her breasts heaved and her blue eyes shot daggers. If looks could kill, he'd be dead on arrival.

Weirdly enough, her anger turned him on. It reminded him of the months she spent trying to ignore him. Still, he was in the wrong and an apology was owed.

"I'm sorry, babe. You're right. I should've called when the meeting spilled over. I drove as fast as I could." He walked to her, each step as careful as if he were approaching a wild animal. He knew any moment she could launch another projectile. With his luck, it would be the stiletto. He didn't want '*Here lies Sergeant Harold Tyler, killed by a fancy spiked heel*' on his epitaph. "Can you forgive me?"

Her blue eyes narrowed. He could see the wheels spinning inside her beautiful head. She wore her hair down, waving softly over her shoulders, just the way he liked it. She'd gone out of her way to look extra-gorgeous, and if his nose didn't deceive him, cooked up something deliciously Italian. He felt like shit. It was the two-month anniversary of the night they reconnected as a couple.

She turned abruptly and stomped into the kitchen. There, she peeled the foil back on the pan of stuffed shells, doling out two onto a plate. The way she plopped them down, splattering the sauce onto the marble countertop told him she was still fuming. He patted his pocket, said a quick prayer, and walked up behind her.

Sliding his arms around her waist, he kissed the nape of her neck. "I really am sorry, Joely. Please don't stay mad. I deserve it, but can't we salvage our night? Please," he whispered against her ear.

Some of her anger drained away. The moment he touched her she forgave him. But she wasn't ready just yet to let it all go. "I spent all day cooking this meal, Harry."

"I know," he said, rubbing his beard along the sensitive skin of her nape.

She let him nuzzle her. "That's not fair," she sighed.

A deep chuckle rumbled from his chest. "All's fair in love and war, baby. I gotta use the tools I have. Don't want to get eaten by an angry lioness."

"It's leopard, not lioness. Not that you noticed."

He slid his hands over her hips, across her flat tummy, and then down over her thighs and back up. "Oh, I noticed. Can't you tell?" He pulled her ass against the burgeoning hardness in his pants.

She smiled, wiggling. "You mean this old thing?"

"Old?" He spun her around.

She laughed. "Well, I don't know. It's been so long since I've seen it, it's surely aged since then."

He growled, grinding against her pelvis. "Since last night you mean? Well, you can check for wrinkles but I'm pretty sure right now you won't find any."

Joely reached down between them, pressing her palm to his rock-hard shaft. He groaned. She grinned. "No more being late without a phone call, right?" She gave him a sexy squeeze.

His eyes rolled back. "No ma'am. I will always call if I'm going to be late."

"Because I need to know if you're not coming."

He grabbed her hips and leaned her back over the counter. "Oh, I'm coming, baby. And so are you. I think dinner can wait a little while longer, don't you?"

"Harry—"

He kissed her, hard. Passions exploded. Tongues tangled and hands roamed wildly. Eastwood reached down for the hem of her dress pulling it up and over her head. With a flick, he undid the clasp of her bra freeing her breasts. His hungry eyes took in the meal he was about to devour.

"Stay just like that," he said, squatting down. On one knee with his prosthetic leg kicked out to one side, he tugged her panties down removing them from first one ankle and then the other. "Keep those on," he said, looking at her stilettos. He looked up at his naked goddess. She stood, lips parted, blonde hair falling over shoulders, breasts peaked. He could smell her excitement.

With deliberate slowness, he parted her thighs and beheld the core of her womanhood. Leaning in, he inhaled. "I'm sorry I was late to dinner. Happy anniversary, baby," he said, then licked her.

Joely gasped. Harry worked her over, licking and sucking her sensitive nub. She was so wet and swollen she thought she'd die. When he slid two fingers inside and rubbed in time to each lick, she felt her climax building. Panting, she gripped the countertop for dear life. It was the best apology she'd ever received.

Eastwood tasted his woman, focusing on the most sensitive part of her until her knees gave and she called his name. He gripped her ass, lifting her up as he continued his lusty assault. Her thighs shook around his ears. Excited beyond control, he stopped, pulling himself up to standing. Joely reached for his fly, unbuttoning and unzipping. Before he could blink, she'd freed his throbbing member.

Turning around, she bent over the counter. "Pull my hair!"

"Damn, I love you," he said, grabbing a fistful of her silky-soft hair and pulling.

"What?" she said.

He entered her, thrusting hard.

"Oh, yes!" she said. "Squeeze my tits, Harry."

"Anything for you, baby," he said, palming her breast and tweaking the nipple.

"Harder!" she pushed back against him.

Eastwood pumped harder, squeezing her tit and pulling her hair. He never knew anyone as wild and abandoned as Joely. Never knew a woman who knew exactly what she wanted. She amazed him every day and that didn't even include how smart this woman was. She was perfect. Perfect for him. He felt his balls tighten and the climax washed over him. Veins stood out in relief on his neck as the intensity took him. Joely screamed, her fingernails desperately trying to claw into the marble.

"Fuck yes!"

Her exclamation was music to his ears. Better than Bach. More soothing than a sonata. He leaned over her, kissing her back, his hands rubbing up her sides and down her arms where he entwined his fingers with hers.

"You are so fucking beautiful."

Joely smiled. "You can't even see me right now," she said, her cheek against the marble, her face hidden beneath a tangle of mussed blonde hair. "I'm just something soft and warm between you and this cold countertop."

"Oh, shit, I'm sorry." He stood, helping her up and spinning her around in his arms. He gazed into her eyes. They glowed like the heavens themselves. With her hair a mess, his handprint still on her breast, and not a stitch of clothing on, she put all other women to shame. He smoothed her tresses back, his thumb caressing her cheek. "I repeat, you, my sweet Joely, are so fucking beautiful."

"Oh, Harry. Is that afterglow talk?" She wrapped her arms around his neck.

"No, it's before-glow, during-glow, AND afterglow talk. It's just the truth, baby."

She kissed him. He returned that kiss, taking his time. It was filled with promise.

Pulling back, he rubbed his nose to hers. "So, now dinner?"

She laughed. "Yes, but let's clean up first. We can't eat stuffed shells with me all sticky and you with your pecker hanging out."

She took his hand leading him to the bathroom. After a quick shower and a lot of kissing and touching, they found themselves sitting on the patio enjoying the cool, fall Nevada night. Somewhere between the dinner and more Sangria, he remembered the package in his pants pocket.

"Hold on, baby." He got up and walked back into the condo.

Joely sipped her wine, wondering for the second time that day if she could ever be any happier than she was at this very moment.

Eastwood came back to the table, but instead of taking his seat, he went down on one knee, left leg kicked out to the side.

"What are you doing," she chuckled.

He took her hands, turning her in the chair to face him. "Since the day we met, there's only been you. Even for those nine months we were apart, I thought about you."

"You didn't date anyone before..." Her eyes showed surprise.

"No one. To be fair, I was overseas, but regardless, since London, the only woman I've been with, Miss Joely Winter, is you. And I'm not the least bit sorry about that. You're amazing. Incredible. A pain in my ass..."

She started to speak, but he cut her off.

"In the best possible way. You make me laugh. You lift me up. You see the best in me even when I'm doubting myself. I look forward to every single day now because I know you're in it. I want that every day for the rest of my life." He paused, pulling a small black velvet box out of his pocket.

Joely's jaw dropped and her eyes misted over. "Harry?"

He opened the box, presenting the princess diamond surrounded by sapphires, set in platinum. "Joely, I love you. Not just when we're," he wiggled his eyebrows, glancing at the kitchen counter, "but in the quiet moments, the difficult ones, and all the other moments in between. You're the one. Will you do me the honor of becoming my wife?"

She tried speaking past the painful lump in her throat but couldn't. He waited, watching her tear up, fearing the worst. Suddenly, she threw her arms around his neck. He felt her head bobbing up and down.

"Is that a yes?" He prayed hard.

"Oh, Harry! Yes! Yes, I'll marry you!"

He engulfed her in a bear hug, relief washing over him, joy filling him. "Oh, baby! Thank you!" He kissed her, once, twice, three times, and held her tight once again. "Oh, my lord, she said yes." He looked out over the patio and screamed, "She said yes!"

A voice coming from one of the condos above answered. "Congratulations."

Joely laughed. Eastwood hooted.

"You are a crazy man, Harold Tyler," she said. "And I love you too, baby."

They gazed at each other, soaking in the happiness. Suddenly, he pulled away, getting up.

"Where are you going, Harry?"

He extended his hand, helping her up and leading the way inside. "I have to call mom. We have to tell her."

Laughing, she followed him in.

He picked up his phone and dialed. "Hello? Mom?" He looked at Joely. "I have some really good news." Grinning, he slid his arm around Joely's waist and pulled her in for another kiss.

EPILOGUE

It was a perfect spring day in April. Eastwood adjusted his tie and straightened his vest. He took a step back and checked himself out in the full-length mirror. The black suit fit well over his chiseled frame. The white shirt and vest were complimented by the blue silk handkerchief in his pocket and the matching blue silk tie. A silver tie pin held it in place. The piece was special, a gift from his team. It was a recreation of their patch but instead of flames, the skull's eyes held two diamond chips. The unit's logo was engraved on the back. Diamond cuff links completed the look. With his beard trimmed close showing off his jawline and fresh haircut, he thought he made quite an impression. He hoped so. The only person's approval he needed was Joely's.

Beside him, Jackson Hicks wore similar attire. His hid the high-tech modified titanium brace that supported his right leg. Despite nearly a year of therapy, nerve damage to the right side still made the stability of his right leg iffy. But you'd never know it. He'd learned to navigate with the brace so well, his limp was almost unnoticeable now. And he had the cool laser-vision prosthetic eye like Art. Watching those two play laser tag was like watching two grown men with toy light sabers. Funny as hell. Jackson had become one of Eastwood's best friends. It was only fitting he should be his best man.

The two men stood inside the dressing room at the Hun-ka-Hunka Burnin' Love Wedding Chapel in Las Vegas, one helping as much as he could, the other sweating bullets, but excited. His unit was out there waiting. Art, Mac, Ben, Nastjia, Matt, and Major Maxwell. Natalie Janeway was there too, the acting maid of honor. His mom had flown in dragging his aunt Ruth with her. Joely's dad, Ralph Winter, came with his plus one, Joely's stepmother. Her mom, Kate, brought her new boyfriend, Julio. Joely's parents were a bit of a shit-show, but they were never boring. He felt bad that more of their loved ones couldn't be invited. With their NDA's, the guest list had to remain within the unit with parents as the exception. Janeway made sure everyone was versed in what they could and could not tell the bride's and groom's parents.

Whatever the case, he was happy. Today, he was marrying the woman he loved. It was going to be a great day.

"Well, buddy, I don't think we can get any more handsome," said Jackson.

The door opened and the chapel wedding coordinator, Derek, poked his head in. "It's time."

Eastwood felt a trickle of sweat glide down into the crack of his ass. He shook his hands, trying to loosen up, and then pulled an extravagant pair of Elvis Presley sunglasses out of his pocket putting them on his face. Jackson did the same. They looked at each other, grinning.

"Let's do this."

Jackson chuckled. "Come on. Time for the King to take the stage."

They followed Derek out into the hall. He took them through another door that led to the altar of the tiny chapel. Eastwood took his place, Jackson next to him. He looked out at the pews and his jaw dropped. A sea of Elvis sunglasses greeted him. Not surprising because that was their theme, but it was all the smiling faces behind them.

His mother Meredith and Aunt Ruth sat in the front pew, both beaming with pride. Behind them were his unit, but it was the other side that floored him bringing tears of joy to his eyes.

Grinning like lunatics were Ghost, Doc and his fiancé Leisl, Hollywood, Skyscraper, and a woman next to Skyscraper that had to be Fatima, his new ladylove, and Outlaw and his wife Emma who held an adorable baby boy—also wearing Elvis sunglasses. As if that wasn't enough, the general himself, P.K. Davidson stood next to Outlaw rocking his King of Rock-n-Roll specs. The smirk on his grizzled countenance counted as a smile.

His heart overflowed with happiness. He was about to walk over and greet them when the music began. Strains of *I Can't Help Falling in Love With You* sung by The King himself filled the small space decorated with Elvis kitsch and red and white roses. Everyone turned.

At the back of the chapel, Natalie Janeway, wearing a shell-pink strapless Versace gown in silk and organdy came down the aisle. The young woman who normally looked like a typical college geek was transformed by Joely and her army of designers and makeup artists. Gone were the glasses and now her big brown eyes with long lashes commanded attention. The dress hugged her petite frame and Eastwood noticed that whatever underthings his lady had chosen for Natalie, it gave her quite the eye-catching cleavage. He glanced at Art. A grin slid across his face. Diaz had noticed too. Things were looking good for their bet.

Natalie took her place at the left side of the altar.

All eyes were glued to the back of the aisle.

Joely came into view, escorted by her father. Eastwood's heart swelled with joy. Next to him, he heard Jackson mutter, "Damn!"

Damn indeed. His gorgeous lady wore a cream lace body-hugging strapless gown. Another Versace creation. In the spirit of their Elvis-themed wedding, she wore her hair teased out into an exact replica of Priscilla Presley's style on the day she wed The King in 1967. And she wore it well. Her beauty blinded him, and it was all he could do not to cry like a baby. He thanked God for his shades because otherwise, everyone would see how blubbery he'd become.

Mr. Winter stood next to his daughter as the wedding host asked, "Who gives this woman to wed this man?"

"I do,' said Ralph.

The host nodded and Mr. Winter placed Joely's hand in Eastwood's. He leaned in and whispered, "I don't care how badass a soldier you are, son. If you ever hurt my little girl, I'll kill you." Then he grinned and patted Eastwood's shoulder.

Jackson chuckled.

Joely looked at her handsome groom. Her eyes were filled with so much love, Eastwood thought he'd drowned happily within their blue depths.

"Hey, baby," he whispered.

"Hey, yourself," she answered.

"You look so fucking beautiful."

The host cleared his throat, smiling. "May I," he interrupted.

The audience laughed.

The ceremony proceeded with the vows, and the giving and receiving of the rings. Joely tried not to giggle when Harry's hand shook so badly, he almost dropped the ring before he could add the platinum band to her stunning engagement ring. Her big, strong fella was nervous.

When he said, 'I do,' his voice wobbled.

Finally, the host pronounced them man and wife.

"You may kiss the bride," he said.

Eastwood didn't need to be told twice. He slid his arms around his beautiful bride dipping her back. To a chorus of "Oohs" and "Ahs," and a round of applause, he kissed his wife for the very first time. It was a kiss full of tenderness, passion, and promise.

"I love you so much, Mrs. Tyler."

Joely grinned, a tear sliding down her face and a blush on her cheeks. "And I love you, my sweet, sexy husband."

The music changed. The upbeat tempo of *A Little Less Conversation* had everyone clapping.

"Ladies and gentlemen, may I present to you, Mr. and Mrs. Harold Tyler."

Eastwood tucked Joely's arm into his and together they danced back down the aisle.

It was a perfect spring day in April, surrounded by family and friends. Standing next to his incredible, sexy, gorgeous wife, Eastwood didn't think he could be any happier. Together they greeted their guests, caught up with old friends, and introduced new ones.

The General shook his hand, and leaning in, said, "I told Outlaw this was your rehab group. No need to say any more than that. Not now, anyhow. Perhaps in the future. I just figured since it was a special day and all..."

Eastwood swallowed past the lump in his throat. That the general thought enough of him to break protocol, just a little bit, to invite his old team to his wedding meant the world to him. "Thank you, sir. I understand, and I really appreciate it."

The general stood tall, formal once again. "Don't make me regret the sentiment, Sergeant. Carry on."

Joely laughed and hugged her husband. Seeing him so humble made her love him more.

Eastwood wiped a tear from his eye and blamed the Nevada dust. He noticed the gift table piled with packages, and remembering, snapped his fingers, pulling a small a pink envelope from his inside jacket pocket. It was wrapped with a bow. He presented it to Joely.

"What's this," she asked, blue eyes wide.

"A little something I picked up here and there." He waited impatiently for her to open it.

Joely pulled the ribbon and opened the envelope. She looked inside, pulling the items out. "Postcards?" She rifled through the small stack, flipping them over and reading the backs.

"For you. One for every place I've been since my first PATCH mission. See," he said, pulling out the first one he'd picked up in Kiev, "I wrote you. Even though I couldn't mail them, I was thinking of you. Just wanted you to know."

Tears welled in her eyes and she swiped at them. "Dammit, Harry, my makeup is going to run down my face. Our wedding pictures will be ruined!"

He chuckled. "There's no way on this earth you could ever take a bad picture, Joely.

She read the back of the first postcard and then threw her arms around his neck, squeezing for all she was worth. "I love you so much, you big sentimental goofball."

"Thank God, because I sure do love you," he said, dropping a kiss on her nose. "Hey, at least we'll have one heck of a story to tell our grandchildren."

She laughed. "Don't put the cart before the horse, Harry. Children first. Then grandchildren."

"Challenge accepted, Mrs. Tyler. How soon can we begin?"

They danced, ate cake, and drank good champagne. This is what life was all about, and he was forever grateful for the second chance that brought him here, that led him to the love of his life. At this moment, life was good.

The End

Also By Michele E. Gwynn

Did you miss books I-V in the Green Beret Series? Grab them now! Rescuing Emma, Loving Leisl, Freeing Fatima, Saving Christmas, and Loving Freddie, newly remastered and re-edited with bonus scenes. The Green Beret series was previously written as part of the special forces world created by NYT Bestselling Author Susan Stoker. The series is now re-edited outside of Stoker's world with an all-new SEAL teams as a point of contact/support team to Outlaw's Green Berets: Visit micheleegwynnauthor.com.

The Soldiers of PATCH-COM is the spinoff series from Gwynn's Green Beret series. Secondhand Soldier is the debut book. Keep up with new releases in this series by signing up for my newsletter.

Checkpoint Novels

Exposed: The Education of Sarah Brown (novel)
The Evolution of Elsa Kreiss (novel)
The Redemption of Joseph Heinz (novel)
The Making of Herman Faust (prequel novella)

Green Beret Series

Rescuing Emma (18+)
Loving Leisl
Freeing Fatima
Saving Christmas
Loving Freddie
Saving Major Morgan (A Green Beret Series prequel novel-
la)

The Soldiers of PATCH-COM

Secondhand Soldier (18+)
Second Chance Soldier
Second Breath Soldier
Silent Night Soldier

C'est la Vie Soldier (Coming Soon)

The Harvest Trilogy

Harvest (audiobook available free on my YouTube channel)
Hybrids
Census

Section 5 (A Harvest Trilogy Spinoff)

Angelic Hosts Series

Camael's Gift (audiobook available on my YouTube channel)
Camael's Battle (audiobook available on my YouTube channel)
Sophie's Wish
Nephilim Rising

Stand Alones

Darkest Communion (Paranormal Romance, 18+)
Waiting a Lifetime (Contemporary Romance, Mystical)
Hiring John (Romantic Comedy 18+)

www.ingramcontent.com/pod-product-compliance
Lightning Source LLC
Chambersburg PA
CBHW021156110726
47900CB00002B/598